CALL OF THE GUN

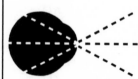

This Large Print Book carries the
Seal of Approval of N.A.V.H.

CALL OF THE GUN

PHIL DUNLAP

WHEELER PUBLISHING
A part of Gale, Cengage Learning

Detroit • New York • San Francisco • New Haven, Conn • Waterville, Maine • London

GALE
CENGAGE Learning™

LIBRARY OF CONGRESS CATALOGING-IN-PUBLICATION DATA

Dunlap, Phil.
    Call of the gun / by Phil Dunlap.
        p. cm. — (Wheeler Publishing large print western)
    ISBN-13: 978-1-59722-742-1 (lg. print : alk. paper)
    ISBN-10: 1-59722-742-0 (lg. print : alk. paper)
        1. Colorado — Fiction. 2. Large type books. I. Title.
    PS3604.U548C35 2008
    813'.6—dc22   2008002704

Published in 2008 by arrangement with Leisure Book, a division of
Dorchester Publishing Co., Inc.

To my wife and family, who generously forgive my intermittent absences from their company, as I sit transformed for hours before the flickering screen of my faithful Macintosh. And to my editor, Abby Holcomb, whose thoughtful insights keep me focused, from beginning to end.

CHAPTER ONE

July, 1877

Saturday nights were smoky, raucous affairs at the Little Nugget Saloon in Lake City, Colorado. Just one of many such establishments in town, the Little Nugget always seemed to have more than its share of thirsty miners intent on spending their wages on gambling, drinking and women — and the Nugget offered all three. On any given night, one could expect to see men exchange angry words, perhaps even a fistfight or two, but seldom did it all come down to a killing — seldom, that is, until one man decided it was time to make his mark on history. Creeg Bedloe, a down-on-his-luck drifter, had been looking forward to this day ever since a firearms peddler arrived in town a couple of months back, bringing with him just what Bedloe saw as a way to cast off his worthless life, and become somebody who commanded notice when he walked down the street.

It was a summer Saturday, around eight in the evening, while the heat of the day still seemed to cling to everything, when Creeg Bedloe pushed through the batwing doors to the saloon with a plan — a plan that would end up with someone dead. He shouldered his way through the rowdy crowd and shouted over the clamor to the bartender for a double whiskey, then squeezed between two men, leaned on the makeshift bar, and turned to strike up a conversation with the man next to him, a young Mexican from one of the nearby mines, who was colorfully garbed for his evening in town.

"Well, ain't you a sight. You're one of them Mex's from up at the Grand Stake, ain't ya?" Bedloe said.

The brim of Bedloe's neatly blocked, flat-crowned hat was pulled down low. He wore a blue striped shirt, no collar, and a vest with silver conchoes on the front. At his side, in a handmade holster hiked up high, was the only thing in the world for which he had any real respect: A brand new, nickel-plated Colt Peacemaker .45 with carved ivory grips, which, to Creeg Bedloe, had emerged as the symbol of his worth as a man. He had scratched together every penny he could get his hands on — much of it ill-gotten — to buy the custom-made Colt from a traveling firearms peddler only a few months earlier. Now that it was his, and his alone, he felt taller, stronger, and suddenly important. In fact, he had all but traded his very soul for the excitement that came over him when his fingers caressed the smooth, gleaming revolver with its six deadly cartridges, just awaiting an opportunity to exact vengeance on his enemies, new or old.

"Sí, señor, I am Juan Estavez. And your name, sir?" The young man removed a rumpled sombrero and held it in front of him. He smiled a big smile, revealing a bright gold tooth in front.

"Creeg Bedloe, you may have heard of me," he said raising one eyebrow. "Let me buy you a drink, Juan."

"Gracias, señor, you are a generous man."

"Bartender, a double for my new friend here." Creeg raised his hand and motioned to the thin, pallid-faced man with slicked down hair, serving drinks from behind a temporary construction consisting of several long, rough-sawn pine boards atop two large wooden barrels. A custom bar had been ordered from St. Louis, but had yet to arrive. The Little Nugget had been open for

9

only three months, just one of many saloons to have sprung up in a town flourishing from the many gold strikes in the vicinity.

A cold, calculating man, Bedloe hadn't suddenly decided to become generous or friendly, for that certainly wasn't a part of his character. Over a period of several weeks he'd paid particular attention to this young miner on many occasions and had gotten to know his habits. He knew what and how much the young man drank, what his limit was, and how far he could be pushed. Creeg had watched this normally quiet man succumb to a quick temper when drinking, and he intended from the start to push him to that point. That was his simple, but deadly plan. And it was now time to put the plan into action.

"I can't help but take a fancy to that vest you're wearin', but with all them silver buttons and eye-poppin' colors, seems you'd attract a lot of attention sneakin' across the Rio Grande," he said matter-of-factly. He didn't even look at the man as he spoke.

The Mexican's eyes narrowed and his nostrils flared at Bedloe's thinly disguised suggestion that he was an uninvited immigrant, not fit to share US soil. "Señor, I did not cross the Río Bravo; I am a citizen of this country, born in Texas," he shot back.

"So you are, so you are. Perhaps I've misjudged you. Well, drink up, and have another on me for the mistake." Bedloe pushed his own double whiskey in front of Juan, who quickly downed the first, then lifted the second with a toasting gesture to Bedloe and just as promptly gulped it down. "My soul, you are a thirsty gent, join me in another before I call it a night. Bartender, two more doubles down here."

Without touching his own drink, Bedloe scrutinized the man's every move. He took note of how quickly the man had taken offense at his transparent insult. It was a test. A test of predictability.

The Mexican's eyes were beginning to glaze as he slung down his third double, then the fourth, again passed along by Bedloe. Since he had not eaten anything since early that morning, the whiskey had an almost immediate effect. His speech thickened, his movements became awkward. Bedloe knew the time was rapidly approaching for him to make his move.

Bedloe leaned forward and said in a low voice only the young man could hear, "You know, Juan, it's too damned bad ol' Sam Houston didn't send all you Sonorans back where you come from when he had the chance."

The man spun around, instinctively dropping his hand to a .36 caliber, JM Cooper Navy Model revolver shoved into his waistband. He blinked repeatedly to clear his blurring vision. His face flushed with anger as he steadied himself with his left hand on the bar. "You make a mockery with your gesture of friendship, señor. I think you are a wolf in the skin of a sheep. Perhaps you wish to consider again about what you have just said."

"Naw, I think maybe I'll just finish what ol' Sam started," Bedloe said, stepping back two steps from the bar, right hand touching the grip of the gleaming Colt.

"Then, may the saints be with you!" the man shouted as he hastily drew his revolver, thumbed back the hammer and raised it in Bedloe's direction with the unsure motion of one unquestionably intoxicated.

Bedloe wasted no time in grasping the opportunity. The other man had drawn first. Creeg Bedloe had been provoked into defending himself, there was no alternative. He drew and fired with the cold, calculating certainty of a man who was stone sober. With a deafening roar, a sudden flash of fire erupted from the muzzle amidst the acrid smell of gun smoke. The bullet plowed into Juan's chest with an awful thud, dropping him to the ground in the blink of an eye. He died almost instantly without even getting off a shot. The seldom fired, rusting Cooper fell harmlessly to the floor from the man's lifeless hand.

When the sheriff came, there were plenty of witnesses to attest to the fact that the dead man had, indeed, drawn first. They all agreed it was solely due to Bedloe's quick action that he was not the man sprawled on the floor in a pool of his own blood. It hadn't gone unnoticed by the sheriff that most of the patrons voicing their support for Bedloe's contention of innocence were also Bedloe's cronies. But without any contradictory evidence, Sheriff Tauber had nothing to hold the gunslinger on.

Bedloe casually sauntered out of the saloon a free man, absolved of blame in the shooting. A prideful smile curled his lips as he ran his hand over the Colt. He felt no remorse, only power.

CHAPTER TWO

September, 1877

One or two of the citizenry claimed to have noticed a distinct odor in the air the day Jeremiah Branson rode into town. The big mountain man sat wearily in the saddle, hunched over slightly as if the journey had been much more than the twenty miles or so down from the high country beyond Slumgullion Pass into the Colorado mining town of Lake City. A broad-brimmed, sweat-stained, slouch hat, sagging and rumpled from years of torturous sun, rain and snow, nearly hid his bearded and weathered face; the buffalo hide-turned-coat gave him the guise of a wild animal come to sniff out the edges of civilization. He was an imposing, if somewhat sorry sight atop the big sorrel mare, and the curious stopped to stare as he dismounted in front of the Little Nugget Saloon. Someone said they were sure the horse gave a sigh of relief as the huge man came off the saddle, pulled a brass-frame Henry rifle from its scabbard, and lumbered across the boardwalk to the saloon. He stopped just inside the tall, pine double doors with the saloon's name lettered right on the glass, looked around a moment to let his eyes adjust to the dark interior, then sought out a solitary table at the far corner of the long, narrow room. He dropped heavily into a captain's chair, with his back to the wall. The rickety old chair creaked under his two hundred and forty pounds.

"What'll it be?" the bartender called to him from across the room, near the end of the crude bar.

"Whiskey. The good stuff. Bring the bottle. And a couple of them eggs in that pickle jar," Jeremiah said as he laid the Henry across the front of the small, round table. He was the only customer. By evening, the place would be packed with gents looking for a good time, and ladies to keep them company. But midday found few with a thirst strong enough to lure them away from the promise of gold and wealth. Those regular revelers who had long since given up such illusions were still sleeping off the night before.

Ten tables, lined up neatly, sat along the

wall opposite the bar, with four to six often mismatched chairs gathered at each. Two faro tables occupied the back of the room, directly under a large, walnut-framed picture of Mr. Lincoln.

Crossing the room in no particular hurry, the bartender put a bottle in front of the stranger, then next to the bottle placed a small plate with two hard-boiled eggs, pickled from days of soaking in vinegar brine.

"Name's Edgar, Edgar Fry, best bartender west of St. Louis. Made them eggs m'self." He wiped his hands on a grimy apron and started to lean on the table. "Ain't seen you 'round here before. You new to these parts?"

"Just whiskey and eggs, no conversation," Jeremiah said in a low, abrupt voice without looking up. The brim of his hat cast a heavy shadow that cut across his face, hiding deep-set, weary eyes. The bartender turned on his heels and returned to his place behind the bar, mumbling to himself about nobody wanting to pass the time of day anymore.

Outside, a thin man wearing a trail slicker who had watched intently as Jeremiah came into town, crossed the dusty street and paused for a moment to look at the sorrel, then noisily entered the saloon. "Whooee, what is that smell? Somebody take a mind to drag in some ol' filthy, flea-infested buffalo hide?" he roared, pointing his nose in the air like a deer sniffing the wind. Creeg Bedloe, Lake City's only self-styled gunfighter, swaggered across the room to the bar and slapped down a single coin. He leaned on the bar, and pulled the slicker back to reveal the gun he carried on his hip.

"Sarsaparilla, *Mr.* Bedloe?" the bartender asked snidely.

"Watch yer tongue! The last man that didn't, ended up with his chest suckin' air." Bedloe reached across the bar, grabbed the scrawny bartender by the collar and yanked him hard, scooting the boards nearly off the barrels.

"Just funnin' you a bit. No need to go gettin' riled," the bartender squealed as he strained against Bedloe's grip, trying to maintain his balance and get his breath.

Bedloe released his hold and pushed the man back hard against several wooden crates that served as the back bar. Glasses clanked against each other from the jostling as the shaken man hastily grabbed for several bottles to keep them from crashing to the floor. *Pushy scoundrel,* the bartender thought, trying to regain his composure. Shakily, he then uncorked a half-filled bottle of pale brown whiskey and poured a shot, spilling half of it as he did. Bedloe quickly downed the drink and impatiently tapped the glass on the bar for another as he glanced around the room.

The only other customer was ignoring the goings-on. He sat forward, elbows on the table, head down in complete silence, occasionally lifting the half-empty bottle to his lips. The distinctive brass and nickel surfaces of the Henry repeater reflected little flashes of light from a flickering oil lamp on the wall, the only illumination in the otherwise dark corner.

Jeremiah Branson, the eldest son of a Welsh immigrant family who had settled in Pennsylvania in 1830, had never liked the East and its crowded cities, so at the end of the War Between the States, he saddled a horse, packed sufficient provisions on two mules to see him through the first winter, and headed west to Colorado for a new way of life. Hunting and trapping became his only means of survival. Changed forever by war, he sought the solitude of the mountains to help him forget the unspeakable slaughter he had seen during that soul-wrenching conflict. It had made an indelible impression on the gentleman — a lasting, dark impression.

Pressed into service with the Pennsylvania Volunteers soon after the first shot was fired on Fort Sumter in '61, he was made a corporal when he proved to have keen eye with a rifle, a talent learned from growing up in the Alleghenys. He saw considerable action on the front lines while lugging a Springfield rifle with a forty-inch barrel, and always gave a good show of himself. He received a commendation at the battle of Stones River while serving under General Rosecrans. After being mustered out as a sergeant in '65, he sought escape from the war's heritage of hatred, and field after field of rotting bodies blown apart by mortar and cannon in numbers so staggering it sometimes took weeks to get them all buried. He rode for the high country to clear his lungs forever of the stench of sulfur, smoke and death.

He felt such a strong revulsion at the inhumanities he'd seen and been a part of, he slunk away from civilization as an atonement for some guilt at having not been killed beside so many of his fellow soldiers. Solitude would from then on be his only companion.

And so, he trapped and hunted alone high in the mountains, with the major threat to his existence coming from an occasional band of Ute Indians that roamed that part of the country. He came down to the several gold or silver mining towns only two or three times a year to trade furs for provisions, to find comfort in watered-down whiskey at a saloon, or perhaps some temporary acceptance with a fancy, sweet-smelling woman making a living off her favors.

Creeg Bedloe was looking for anything but solitude; he dreamed of fame and fortune as a gunfighter. Disillusioned with living a life of one failure after another, having been totally unsuccessful at finding enough placer gold even to fill his pouch, he sought to find a way out of Lake City. To his narrow, twisted mind that way was with a gun. A gun could get a man in his situation a reputation, and a reputation could be turned into cash money in New Mexico where he heard some of the big cattle outfits could always find a place for a man with a gun. If he came with a reputation, so much the better. There was often big money paid to a man with a talent for special kinds of services. Just holding the Colt in his hand fueled his growing obsession with gaining a reputation as a gunman. He needed a name for himself, then he could strike out for someplace like Lincoln County — and some real money. That's why he had invested all he could beg, borrow, or steal into the purchase of the .45 caliber, nickel-plated Colt Peacemaker with which he had recently killed his second victim, another unsuspecting fool easily suckered into a six-gun duel, and too drunk to know what he was doing. Bedloe had been careful to ensure that both had been killed in front of witnesses willing to attest to his self-defense plea when the sheriff came along. Little was said about him plying them both with generous amounts of liquor, though they each had a reputation for being mean drunks who could, if given the slightest incentive, be easily drawn into a fight. Neither of them disappointed him and both were quickly dispatched by his well-oiled, prized Colt, one of the first of its kind seen in Colorado. Rare, too, was the distinctive ivory inlay in the center of the grips, carved in the shape of a rattlesnake with ruby eyes, coiled and ready to strike.

That foul-smelling, unshaven hulk in the corner might just be number three, Bedloe thought. He was struck by the looks of the mountain man from the moment he saw him get down off the big mare. He gave the appearance of being an easy victim. He'd be Bedloe's next victim, and that might be enough dead men to get Bedloe recognized in New Mexico as a good man with a gun.

Bedloe slid his glass around on the unfinished planks, drawing little circles in the spilled whiskey, planning. His scheme would require more witnesses than just this untrustworthy bartender, and he'd need to conjure a way of pushing the odoriferous stranger into a face-off. Bedloe stood sizing up the silent giant. The man carried no sidearm, only a rifle and a leg knife. Bedloe had no doubts he could draw and fire his .45 before a clumsy hulk like this one could get that bulky rifle up, chamber a round, take aim and shoot. Yes, the confrontation would be easy. He had only to formulate a plan. He threw back his head and downed the last drop from his glass, tossed it smartly to the man behind the bar, and strode purposefully toward the door, stopping briefly to take one more sneering look at Jeremiah.

CHAPTER THREE

In the gold camps of Colorado in the early '70s, real law was a rare commodity. But until the Bunot Treaty of '74 eased their fears, the miners' biggest concern was having their hair lifted prematurely by the Utes. After the treaty, the valley opened up to scores of men seeking their fortunes in the streams and riverbeds that snaked down from the high country, created by the melting snows and mountain rains. Lake City, no different from a dozen other hastily constructed towns with exploding populations, was built of native stone, green timber and, quite often, thousands of square feet of canvas. As the numbers of restless men descending on the rapidly expanding town increased — all seeking a temporary reprieve from the hard and uncertain work of the goldfields — the need for law and order quickly became evident. The number of saloons and brothels increased tenfold and keeping the peace required a man of strength, slow to anger, and cool-headed in situations where whiskey was the real malefactor and some misguided miner merely the beneficiary of its influence. Many an average man, sane by day, wound up in a pine box after being bitten by the red-eyed snake, dispensed liberally in any saloon along the wide, dusty main street of Lake City.

John C. Tauber was elected sheriff because he was notably honest, reasonably adept with firearms, slow to anger, and the worst miner within twenty miles of Henson Creek. A tall, rangy man, slightly stooped at the shoulders, he carried a long, afflicted scar down his left cheek, the result of an altercation with a drunken miner wielding a bowie knife. The miner spent three days in jail, paid a $50 fine, then returned to his claim undaunted. Tauber would carry the angry scar for life.

The sheriff had never had to kill a man, but, of late, his concern over Creeg Bedloe and his fancy six-shooter had grown. He hadn't liked the misfit from the first time he laid eyes on him. The growing menace of Bedloe's confidence in his own abilities with that gun was sure to become Tauber's nightmare. Of this, the sheriff was certain.

He had just stepped out of his office door when he saw Bedloe saunter from the Little Nugget, laughing loudly as he approached a small group of men in front of the livery. The sheriff also walked toward the group.

"I swear on my mother's grave it's true; there's a bear in there, or at least it smells like one." Bedloe bellowed and the group joined in. "Looks like a mean one, jus' sittin' there invitin' flies." They all roared again, slapping each other and holding their noses. The sheriff pushed his way into the center of the crowd. He looked Bedloe straight in the cold, green eyes set deeply in a long, gaunt face. Bedloe's high cheekbones and thin lips reminded Tauber of a corpse, something he'd seen plenty of in the rough mining towns during the 1870s.

"What's all the excitement, boys?" the sheriff asked.

Ezra Goode spoke up first. "Why Bedloe here says they's a bear in the bar." Everyone nearly fell over howling, grabbing their stomachs and stomping at the ground.

"What ol' Goode here means is, there's a gent in the saloon that smells a heap like a bear. And I suspect he's up to no good, Sheriff." Bedloe raised one eyebrow and snickered into his fist.

"Well, why don't you boys find something worthwhile to do, and I'll go tend to the bear," Tauber said, as he made a shooing motion with his hand. "Go on, break it up now." The group slowly began to split up, mumbling and snickering to themselves, going off in groups of two or three. All except Bedloe. He tagged along behind the sheriff for a few dozen steps, then decided to roost on the hitching rail outside the saloon. Tauber glanced back over his shoulder as he stepped through the doors to the dark barroom, just to make sure he hadn't collected any of the curious.

"What'll it be Sheriff?" The little man behind the bar was wiping the top of the bar with a filthy rag, stained with beer and whiskey from months of use.

"Beer. That whiskey of yours exasperates my ague."

The bartender snickered as he drew a glass of the warm brew. He slid it across the bar in front of the sheriff, whose eyes were on the silent man in the corner.

Tauber lifted the glass and blew the head of foam onto the floor, leaned across the bar and whispered, "That feller in the corner act like he's lookin' fer trouble?"

"No, Sheriff, he ain't hardly made a sound. Not real talkative," the bartender whispered back.

Tauber nodded, then strolled over to the table where Jeremiah sat. "I'm Sheriff John Tauber, mind if I join you?"

"Do whatever you've a mind to, it's your town," Jeremiah said as he looked up only with his eyes at first, then leaned back in the flimsy chair.

The sheriff removed his narrow-brimmed hat, laid it on the table and scooted the second chair around with the toe of his boot. He eased down slowly, sipping from the beer glass as he did. "You ever see that tall fella before that was in here earlier?"

"Nope," Jeremiah answered with a gravelly voice.

"He say anything to you?"

"Nope."

"You say anythin' to him?"

"Nope."

"Well then, I think we got ourselves a problem." Tauber took another drink from his glass, then, setting it noisily on the table, he wiped his mouth on his coatsleeve. "His name is Creeg Bedloe, and I figure he's aimin' to taunt you. He'd like nothing better than to get you riled up enough to fight. Then he'll gun you down, like he has two others in the last two months. He's a mean one, that Bedloe. Fancies himself a real gunslinger. And he likes to make his own odds."

"Hmm," Jeremiah grunted. "I've known men like him before."

"Sure, we all have. But few of them have this man's deadly intentions. When he gets set on killin', it seems to come to pass. I'd not like to see that happen to you," Tauber said.

"I only plan to be in town for a couple of days. I can stay out of his way," Jeremiah said.

"Easier said than done, friend."

"What is it you're askin' of me?"

"If I was you, I'd slip quietly out the back right now and head back up into them mountains where you come from. I could easy bring your horse around. Nobody'd be the wiser." Tauber stared at the big man, waiting for an agreement. None came.

"Got no reason to run, never run in my life, not from anything nor anybody." Jeremiah's dark, gray eyes narrowed as he thought back on the many times he'd liked to have run, with hundreds of Johnny Rebs screaming and hollering as they came across fields of grass like a plague of locusts. But, he didn't run, even when fear gripped him like a bear trap, he didn't run. He always stood his ground and that wasn't going to change now.

"But I tell you he's a killer lookin' to earn a reputation with that fancy gun of his." The sheriff leaned forward. "There ain't much I can do 'til he makes a move, then it'll probably be too late. Do you understand what I'm sayin', mister, uh . . . I reckon I failed to catch yer name."

"Branson. Jeremiah Branson."

"Mr. Branson, I hope you'll reconsider what I've suggested." Sheriff Tauber stood up, pushed the chair back, and started for the door. "If you choose to stay, I'd suggest avoiding contact with Mr. Bedloe at all costs. Good luck, Mr. Branson." He strode out into the chill autumn air, pulled the lapels of his coat together and stepped off the walk into the street. The glass rattled in the doors as they closed behind him. Bedloe was still there, still perched atop the hitching rail, grinning like a man on a high lonesome.

"That ol' bear take a bite outta you, Sheriff?" Bedloe laughed as he swung his leg over and came off the rail, kicking up dust as he did.

"Creeg, that man in there ain't lookin' fer no trouble. Best you leave him alone or I might have to step in and stop whatever it is you've got a mind to do," the sheriff said to

Bedloe as he passed him, neither stopping nor looking up. He wanted Bedloe to get the idea, but not have a chance to make an issue of it there in the street. Bedloe just smiled and patted the Colt hiked up high on his hip.

Tauber's thoughts were those of a man searching for simple answers to age-old problems as he directed his steps toward his small, one-room office and jail; there must surely be a way to rid the town forever of Creeg Bedloe and his type. The country had gone loco with gold fever, and greed had overcome any sense to be made of it all. Men killing each other over a few ounces of gold flakes, or sometimes just for the sport, simply drew no rational purpose. But he was faced with a different type of man, now. A man who killed not for gold, but for self-esteem, a deep-seated inner need to be recognized and deemed important. That kind of man could only be dealt with one way. He shuddered at the thought that he ultimately might be drawn into conflict with Bedloe to save another man's life. For perhaps the first time, he wished he had not taken the job as sheriff. He wished he was still on the family farm in Ohio, raising pigs with his father.

CHAPTER FOUR

As a deep red sun slid beneath the hills, Bedloe watched the Little Nugget from across the street, seated in the shadows on a bench in front of the sutler's store. He was waiting for the saloon to fill with sufficient patrons keeping the double doors swinging to allow him to re-enter, size up his prey, and make his move should the opportunity arise. He had a feeling about this mountain man. He firmly believed the brooding giant was a man who'd easily be provoked into going for that rifle. He smiled at his own thoughts, playing the scene over and over in his mind. The ending was always the same, with Creeg Bedloe the victor . . . of course. The more he thought, the more he relished the idea of making his own opportunity, forcing the showdown on his terms. It had worked before. It would again. He ran his fingers over the smooth grips of the Peacemaker. He was confident. Ready.

The street itself seemed to rattle and quake from overburdened wagons, struggling through foot-deep ruts left by drenching rains two days before. The mud was gone, leaving the dirt cracked and dry. Swirling dust had now returned, but not before nature had re-sculptured the heavily traveled route to and from the mines. Each time the rains came, the road changed from passageway to quagmire, then back again as the sun reappeared to bake it into a usable surface once more.

The time had come. Bedloe took a deep breath and arose from the bench to make his way through the proliferation of wagons and people to the saloon where he hoped to add the third victim to his total. Smoke and noise greeted him upon entering the bar. As he brusquely shoved aside two near-drunk patrons, he made a place for himself where he could watch and size up the big man in the corner.

Jeremiah sensed Bedloe's return to the dimly lit room, even though a wild confusion of voices filled every inch of space. He did not look up, but instead chose to ignore the man the sheriff had warned him about. Since he now knew what the lanky stranger with the gleaming six-shooter was about, he had decided that what the sheriff suggested made good sense. He would ignore this arrogant, boastful lout at all costs. It was a plan born not solely of self-protection but, also, of a belief that such a man, attempting to climb a mountain too fast, nearly always creates his own avalanche. Bedloe wouldn't be the first man he'd seen crumble under his own temper when failing to get his way. But, just in case Bedloe proved to be something more than expected, Jeremiah slowly placed his hand over the Henry's breach, moving the hammer back until he heard it click into full cock — a subtle action that went unnoticed by Bedloe, who had finally decided the time was right to make his move, to test the mettle of the big man seated alone.

"Policy hereabouts is for strangers to always buy a round fer the house," Bedloe said as he sauntered up to lean on a post near Jeremiah's table. "Of course, if you ain't up to it, we'll just figure you think we're beneath you. That the way it is, Buffalo Man?"

Jeremiah didn't look up. Instead, he slowly poured another drink for himself from the near-empty bottle, and took a sip. The din of the bar began to dissipate as Bedloe got no reaction from his question, and others grew curious as to the outcome of the gunman's prodding.

"Reckon tha's the way it is, folks, this gentleman has come all the way down from them mountains to say he's too good to drink with us rabble," Bedloe said with a snort, then glanced about the room with a questioning look, inviting comments. After a brief silence, during which several of the patrons turned back to their card games or their drinking, a voice came from the other end of the bar. One of Creeg's cronies, Ezra Goode, shouted, "Tha's the way I see it! Best we all go on home, leave the gent to the onliest company he appreciates: Hisself."

"I for one cain't leave," Bedloe quickly said, "as I am surely drawn to linger a bit by the overwhelmin' scent of buffalo perfume. Once drawn to its pleasin' odor, a body can hardly break away." He threw back his head and roared.

Uneasy laughter drifted momentarily throughout the room. Still, Jeremiah gave not the slightest hint of reaction. Bedloe pulled back the slicker to reveal the Colt that hung by his side. "Bet you'd like to throw down on me with that ol' Henry, wouldn't you? Maybe put a bullet in my head?" Bedloe was suddenly aware that his voice had become louder, more excited, and the room had grown dead silent. Nervously his eyes darted about, seeking assurance of some kind from others in the saloon, some popular agreement with his pushing the stranger to a point of confrontation. He saw none. Perspiration now began to trickle down his forehead and he felt awkward, out of place, but he was now committed. "I can see you've no stomach for this. Guess cowards just grow bigger in them mountains," he taunted.

The sound of the doors rattling broke the silence as Sheriff Tauber walked in. Realizing instantly that Bedloe had finally gotten himself in too deep to walk away, he moved quickly to defuse the situation. "Nine o'clock, time for a round on the house; amble up to the bar, boys," the sheriff said with authority. "You don't mind, do you, Edgar?"

"N-no sir," the bartender sputtered, scooping up glasses from the back bar, dirty or clean.

Everyone in the Little Nugget that night hurried to be first at the bar. Bedloe was left without an audience, nearly knocked off balance several times by men, already too drunk to walk a straight line, rushing to get their share of the handout. The bartender, too, had been caught off guard although he'd quickly grasped the significance of the sheriff's expeditious solution to a situation that was rapidly getting out of hand.

Jeremiah rose from his table and slipped quietly from the saloon without Bedloe's notice. When he looked around, he saw his prey had vanished.

"Looks like you lost your 'bear,' Bedloe," said Tauber. The saloon erupted in laughter.

Bedloe spun around and shoved his way through the crowd, straight for the door and out into the cool, night air. He took a deep breath and hurried down the street, stumbling now and again in the hardened wagon ruts that criss-crossed each other like the coarse weave of burlap. Anger and embarrassment nearly overwhelmed him.

Creeg Bedloe let the door slam behind him as he entered the small room in the back of Mrs. Granville's boarding house where he lived: Four walls, a single, narrow iron bed with a well-used feather mattress, a small stand with a wash basin and water pitcher, a tiny, oval mirror hanging on the wall above the stand, and four metal hooks nailed to a board on the wall for his clothes. That was all he had for living quarters; his life's belongings resided in that eight-by-nine room with him. There was nothing else, not even a window. It was cramped, but all he could afford, as he worked very little, seeking out odd jobs as necessary to keep himself alive.

His needs weren't great, and as long as he had food, a place to sleep, and enough left over to buy cartridges for the Colt, he preferred not to work because it cut too deeply into his shooting practice, which he undertook daily at the edge of town near the dump. He was deeply depressed and agitated by the evening's goings-on. He would have preferred getting the stranger riled quickly, making a confrontation simple and easy. That was his plan. Now, that was all changed.

He stared at himself in the tiny mirror, certain he would have come out on top of any gunplay. After all, how could such a clumsy oaf of a man ever match up with Creeg Bedloe, a man who'd already killed two men? A gunfighter. And someday, he'd be one of the best.

He dreamed how it would all go, smooth and easy. But the mountain man had proven to be stubborn, and then that damn sheriff had to butt in. Now, he needed to plan his next move, and maybe, with a little luck, the sheriff would get in his way and end up being number four. Yes, number four, that was a nice round number and killing a sheriff was certain to bump his reputation a notch. Those land barons in New Mexico would be impressed. He saw it all begin to happen right before his eyes in that dark, cramped room.

He fell back on the feather mattress, the springs squeaked a small complaint, then he reached back over his head to grab the bars on the iron bed. As he tugged at them, he lay glaring restlessly at the ceiling.

Distracted by his failure to push Jeremiah into a fight, he felt like a child who'd been punished for some great misdeed. A mixture of self-recrimination and anger put his nerves on edge. He was startled by the sharp knock at his door. He grabbed for the Colt.

"Who is it?" he demanded, perturbed that anyone would disturb him in his humiliation. He didn't want to see anybody.

"Ezra! Kin I come in?" the old man shouted, pushing the door open without waiting for an invitation.

Ezra Goode was the closest thing Bedloe had to a friend in this world. A man cut from the same rotten cloth as the pistolero who fancied himself another John Wesley Hardin.

"Whadda you want, Ezra? I ain't lookin'

for company."

"Why didn't you just up and gun that big man down?" Ezra asked excitedly.

"Because he wouldn't go for that rifle of his. He had to reach for that piece first or the sheriff'd haul my carcass off for a necktie party. That's why, you stupid old man."

"No need to go gettin' nasty, I'm on your side. Maybe he just needs more proddin'," Ezra said.

"With Tauber sniffin' around, it ain't likely I'll get the chance. That sheriff needs dealin' with first," Bedloe said as he slapped his hand down on the bed angrily, raising a dust.

"What's the matter with you? That mountain man ain't important enough to go gettin' yourself shot over."

"I gotta get that sheriff outta the way. Don't you understand? That big man plain ignored me. Nobody ignores Creeg Bedloe and lives. That's why he's important. And that damned Tauber has put himself between me and my standin' over that buffalo's carcass with a hunk of my lead in him." Bedloe gritted his teeth. His eyes narrowed at the picture he'd painted of his dreamed-of triumph.

"So, how do you plan to get Tauber to

leave you alone? He's no fool, you know. He knows what you're up to, now." The old man reached into his tattered vest pocket and pulled out a hunk of chewing tobacco wrapped in waxed paper. He bit off a chunk and wrapped the rest back up.

"I know. That's why I've got to deal with him first!" Bedloe still had the Colt in his hand, though it hung at his side. He raised it up and rubbed its smooth, shiny surface with his other hand. Just holding that gun made him feel stronger, abler.

"How about I help?" Ezra said. Eagerly, he hoped Bedloe would accept his offer. He liked the idea of having someone in his debt. Someday it would come in handy.

"No! Just you get on outta here. Leave me to my plannin'. Go on, now. Git!" Bedloe waved the Colt in the air, hoping the idea of having a gun in his face would discourage the old man from hanging around any longer. Bedloe needed to be alone. Whatever plan he finally settled on, it had to be his and only his. That was important.

The old man grumbled as he hastily closed the door behind him, clumping down the darkened hall to leave the boarding house by the back entrance.

Bedloe concluded he would have to even the odds with the sheriff first, then handle the mountain man afterwards. He knew that face-to-face, he might not have the edge with Tauber, though he'd never seen him shoot. The town board considered him to be a fair shot when they elected him sheriff. That little doubt could give Tauber the edge. There had to be a way. He knew the sheriff would be making his rounds to check the doors and windows of all the shops up and down the main street, and some of the side streets, too, where half the buildings were simply tents or crudely constructed lean-to's. That's what he'd do. He'd wait until midnight, when the sheriff made his late rounds.

He picked up a worn paperback book that lay on the floor next to his bed. It was a book written by an eastern journalist who could make stories of famous gunfighters come alive, create heroes of men who probably didn't deserve more than a mention in some small town newspaper. But, to Creeg Bedloe, it was the bible on how to be a somebody. That's why he bought the gun. And why he bought the silver conchoes from a man who came through town on his way up from Texas to the gold fields. He learned from the book that to be a gunfighter, a man had to be fast, cold, and look the part. Looking the part was very important to Creeg Bedloe, that's why he wore those conchoes on his vest. Very impressive.

CHAPTER FIVE

Because of the lateness of the hour, and because he'd consumed an entire bottle of whiskey, Jeremiah decided to stay the night in town. He stopped the first man on the street he came to after leaving the saloon.

"Where can a man bed down for the night, some place cheap?" he asked.

"Well, sir, there's not much in the way of accommodations, mainly just the hotel down the street. If you ain't real particular, the livery stable's got a purty dry loft, and ol' Simon Stover would welcome the company.

"Gotta put the mare up anyway, might as well," Jeremiah said as he touched the brim of his hat. "Obliged."

He gently ran a rugged hand over the sorrel's nose, then took the reins and walked the big horse slowly down the street to Simon Stover's Livery and Horse Rental. He breathed deeply of the fresh air. It was good to be away from the din of the saloon. The night was cool and still. Only the occasional barking of a dog broke the silence.

One of the large doors at the front of the livery barn was open and Jeremiah led his horse inside the dimly lit barn. Along either side of the building were stalls, each with a small feed trough, a bucket hanging on a peg for water, and ample straw on the floor. Out back, several horses milled about in the corral.

"Kin I help you, sir?" came a voice from the loft above. Jeremiah looked up to see an old man swing around an upright beam and start down a rickety ladder near where he stood. "Be right down."

"I'll be needin' a place to bed my horse and me for the night," Jeremiah said.

"Got just the place for yer horse, but you'd be a might more comfortable at the Gold Claim down the street."

"The Gold Claim?"

"The hotel, at the end of the street," Simon said, wheezing to catch his breath from the climb down the long ladder. "They got some of them new shiny brass beds all the way from St. Louis."

"Well, I'm none too comfortable sleepin' in a bed. I'd be jus' fine on some straw if you could see your way to let me bed down here."

"Glad to have you, no charge, neither." Simon reached to take the reins from Jeremiah. He led the big mare into a stall and called to Johnny, the stable boy, to fetch some grain. "Be two bits for the night for the mare, fed and curried."

"That'll be fine, thanks." Jeremiah pulled a small coin purse from an inside pocket of his buffalo coat, fished around for the right amount, and handed it to Simon.

"You can throw yer bedroll down anywhere you've a mind to," Simon said, making a grand sweeping gesture to let the big man feel at home.

Jeremiah grunted and, without another word, began to untie two heavy, six-point wool blankets from the back of his saddle. He threw them down just outside a stall, gathering some straw under one end as a makeshift pillow as Simon sauntered off towards the front to close the door.

The night wind began to whistle through the side walls of the drafty barn, winds that would bring the chill of autumn down through the valley. Jeremiah's thoughts turned to his small cabin up high among the peaks and spires of the mighty Rockies, and the warmth of evenings in front of the stone fireplace. Nestled in a stand of Ponderosa pines, near the tree line on the leeward side of rocky cliffs on a lush, grassy knoll, the cabin was protected from the fierce winter winds that screamed down from the north, but fell victim to immense snows, dumped all winter and well into the spring on the eastern slopes. Even when snowfall nearly covered the cabin, leaving little more than the roof and chimney exposed, his appreciation of the power and beauty of the high mountains gave him the strength to endure the long, brutal winters.

A thick, bushy beard, with a mustache starting to curl at the corners of his mouth, hung below a sharply chiseled nose; heavy, dark eyebrows loomed like brooding buzzards over the deep-set, steel-gray eyes. He stood six-feet-four and, with broad shoulders and a barrel chest, towered over most men, which went a long way toward discouraging most tormentors concerned with his lack of stylish attire. He journeyed down from his mountain retreat only occasionally, not seeking the companionship of other men, but as a way to temporarily reattach himself to the real world, a world of greed and ugliness he couldn't allow himself the luxury of forgetting. To Jeremiah, forgetting would be a betrayal of all the lives of friends he had seen snuffed out by man at his worst during that cruel War Between the States.

The lives he had taken had in no way evened the score, yet still they weighed heavily on his conscience, for killing a complete stranger went entirely against his grain. During the war, he often felt trapped between conscience and duty. His strong sense of duty had proven to outweigh all else. But this inner turmoil had driven him after the war to seek shelter from a world he didn't really understand and didn't want to be a part of.

He drifted off into a fitful sleep wondering if a man like Creeg Bedloe ever wrestled with his conscience or found himself bedeviled by having a talent for killing.

Sheriff Tauber stepped from his office door into the dark, chill of the night. It was time to make his rounds, to make sure that none of the stores had been broken into or no drunk, sleeping off too many overpriced whiskeys, lay crumpled in someone's doorway. It was also a time to think, perhaps to come up with a plan to solve the Creeg Bedloe dilemma without someone getting killed, though that looked increasingly unavoidable.

He walked casually along the wooden

sidewalk that ran the length of the town, stopping at each store or office to check the doors and windows, rattle the doorknobs, and listen for sounds of prowlers or mischief makers. He had just come around the stone meeting hall when he heard a sound near the livery stable, the sound of something or somebody poking about among the crates in the alley between the two buildings. The night was nearly pitch black. An overcast hid the moon and no light shone from any windows into the alley. All he could see were vague shadows.

"This is the sheriff, who's there?" There was no answer, but the sound stopped. He waited for a moment, then started down the alley. He strained to see movement or to hear anything more of the sound that brought him there in the first place. Nothing. Must have been a stray dog searching through the trash for a free morsel, he thought. He turned to retreat back to the street. At that instant, when his guard was down, a shadowy figure silently rose from behind one of the crates. The sheriff was struck a blow from behind that buckled his knees and sent him sprawling face down on the ground. Momentarily, the figure stood over the unconscious man, then, raising his boot heel, stomped down hard on the sheriff's limp right hand. A dull thud and the snap of breaking bones was the only sound heard. The figure ran from the alley and disappeared into the darkness.

Soon afterward, Jeremiah, unable to sleep soundly, was awakened by the sound of moaning coming from outside the barn. Getting up to investigate, he took an oil lamp that hung on a peg by the door, struck a match, and held it to the wick. It gave sufficient light to guide him, and he slipped quietly out a side door. There, just outside, he found the sheriff coming to, struggling to shake off the effects of the blow to his head. Jeremiah lifted the helpless man to his feet, then half-dragged, half-carried him inside. He helped him to a pile of straw and brought some water from the trough at the back of the barn.

"What happened?" he asked, as the sheriff, still groggy, eagerly took the cup of water.

"I . . . don't know . . . just . . . went to investigate a sound . . . must have been hit from behind." Then the pain from the mangled hand came through the mist of his returning memory. "Ohh, damn, my hand . . . it feels broken."

"Looks like. We better get a doc to patch you up," Jeremiah said as he started to stand. Tauber reached out to him.

"The new doc won't be here for a month . . . just help me wrap it."

"Okay, but you really need a doc." Jeremiah slipped his bowie knife from its sheath shoved down inside his high boot and cut two short lengths of heavy rawhide from a large piece that hung over one of the stalls. Then he took a shirt from one of his saddlebags and cut a piece off the tail. He placed squares of the stiff leather on either side of the mangled hand, wrapping and tying it tightly with the length of shirt, straightening the twisted fingers as best he could. Tauber gritted his teeth and held his breath, nearly passing out from the pain. When Jeremiah had finished, he fashioned a sling from a length of rope.

"Thanks," Tauber said as he tried without success to get to his feet. "Would you help me back to the jail?"

Jeremiah lifted the man up onto the back of the sorrel and led the big horse through the creaky double doors and down the two blocks to the jail. Once there, he slung a massive arm around the sheriff and carried him inside to a bunk in one of the cells. Jeremiah lit a lamp and pulled a chair up beside the bunk.

"Where'd you come from?" Tauber asked. He held his throbbing hand. Jeremiah had placed a wet cloth over the ugly wound to help ease the pain and bring down some of the swelling after he'd cleaned the blood from the gash left by the blow to the back of Tauber's head.

"The livery. I was bedded down inside," Jeremiah answered.

"That's not what I meant. I ain't never seen you around here before today. You got a cabin nearby?" Tauber asked, pursuing that ever present need of a lawman to ask questions, even if it meant talking through the agony he was suffering.

"Northeast of here, 'bout two days' ride," Jeremiah nodded.

"How about before that. Where was you raised?" Tauber found himself intrigued by the quiet stranger that had helped him. He wanted to know what he was all about.

"Pennsylvania, a farm."

"You serve in the war?" Tauber continued.

"Pennsylvania Volunteers."

"What were you, infantry?"

"They stuck me in the lines with a rifle, and told me to shoot anyone in gray that had fancy braid on their jacket. I did. Why do you ask?"

"You remind me a mite of my brother. And, I just got a feelin' you're good with that Henry. It was thanks to men like you

51

that my brother is still alive. He stuck his head up along a line just as a cavalry officer started to jump the picket with his horse. He was close enough to run ol' Billy through with his saber when a man cut that officer down like a tin can off a stump. Maybe it was you that done it. Whoever it was, I'm mighty grateful. You gotta be damn proud of the job you done."

"I never could get used to shootin' a man down and not knowin' a lick about him, whether he was good, or bad, or had a family that loved him, or children."

"Reckon I can understand. Knowin' whether the man is good or bad might make a difference. I always figured it was a bad one that nearly killed my brother."

"Maybe," Jeremiah muttered. "It musta been a bad one that did this to you too. Who was it?"

"Probably Creeg Bedloe . . . so I couldn't stop him from goadin' you into a fight."

"Then you better let me help, you're in no condition to take him on," Jeremiah pleaded.

"Nope. It's my job, an' I'll tend to him come mornin'," Tauber answered. He desperately needed help and he knew it, but whatever it is that makes a man shy away from asking for it — pride, ego or just plain stubbornness — was in full charge and the sheriff would not relent. The pain was taking its toll and weariness finally overcame him. He closed his eyes. Jeremiah drew a blanket up over him, then doused the lamp as he left.

CHAPTER SIX

The morning dawned gray and overcast, with a damp coolness in the air as Tauber stepped into the wagon-rutted street, his right hand still wrapped in the crude bandage from Jeremiah's old shirt. In his left hand he carried a 44-40 Winchester carbine. He looked up toward the livery, then down toward the saloon; there, as he suspected, was Bedloe, leaning against a porch post in front of Carter's Dry Goods, three buildings up from the Little Nugget. Tauber had made a decision. He had to put an end to Bedloe's plotting to kill innocent men for his own gain. The time had come to make a stand.

"Bedloe, you're under arrest!" he shouted.

"For whut?"

"Stirrin' up trouble, incitin' to riot, public drunkenness, maybe breakin' a man's hand . . . hell, I don't know, I'll think of somethin', but you're going to spend some time in jail. Now, are you going to make this easy or hard?"

"Ha! Hear that everybody, this washed-up nobody is gonna put me, Creeg Bedloe, in jail fer he don't know what."

He grabbed the post and swung around like a kid swinging on a fence. Twice, three times around. Then he stopped and stepped off the porch into the street, tugging at the bottom of his leather vest with the four Spanish silver conchoes on the front. He was dressed just as the writer had instructed. He looked like a somebody. He appeared on the street clean shaven with his hair slicked down, smelling of bay rum, and wearing a clean shirt.

"Hey, all you fine citizens of Lake City, c'mon out! Come see the show! Looks like a good day for someone to die, don't you think, Sheriff?" Bedloe shouted at the top of his lungs. He must have an audience. He had grown to feel a strange need, a need for the adulation of onlookers. He was becoming a showman. Bedloe and his fancy gun.

Tauber stood with his feet firmly planted about a boot length apart. He didn't move or say anything. He could feel only the throbbing pain run up his arm from his crushed hand. Tending properly to the hand would have to wait. His heart was beating

55

like a Comanche drum and he felt a lump in his throat. He was scared, scared that *he* would be the one to die that day. He didn't want to die, but he was in a situation that allowed only one other way out: To run, run for his life, and never stop running. He knew that's what it would be. A coward never ceases running, for that *becomes* his life. So, while he thought his heart would burst from fear, he couldn't take that first step toward escape. That would be, to Sheriff John C. Tauber, no escape at all. However, for that moment, he wished he'd accepted the mountain man's offer of help.

"You fixin' to face me down with a rifle, Sheriff One-hand?" Bedloe danced around once, kicking up dust as he went, laughing the vicious laugh of a tormented clown.

Watching these antics, Tauber now knew it had been Bedloe who'd bushwhacked him in the alley. He could see it in the man's eyes, hear it in his voice. And now, he, too, realized he'd been set up like the others. Led into a trap, having to overcome some infirmity. He hadn't been tricked into consuming too much senses-depriving whiskey as had the others, but something just as devious. He'd been drawn into that alley. It was Bedloe's trademark to slant the odds in his own favor. It looked like it had worked again.

Hearing the commotion, curious onlookers began to emerge from the shops and houses up and down the street. It was obvious something was going to happen, and soon. No one gave any thought to the possibility of catching a stray bullet. They gathered like vultures on the boardwalk, in windows, and along the perimeter of the street. This would be something to see. A real gunfight. Would they soon be without a sheriff, or would this be the day that the arrogant bully Bedloe finally got what was coming to him? Somewhere amongst the crowd, bets were surely being placed.

"It's time Sheriff, it's your move. You're gonna have to shoot to take me, because I ain't goin' to no jail. You got no cause to take me in." He dropped his hand to his side, he could feel the carved grip of the Colt brush his anxious fingers. He felt a rush of excitement.

Tauber knew he had to make the first move. He didn't like it, but with that broken hand he didn't stand a chance if he didn't. He'd have to raise the muzzle of the Winchester, slip his battered arm under the barrel to balance and help aim, then fire with deadly accuracy. He would have no chance to re-chamber a cartridge if he missed.

Beads of sweat covered his forehead, even though a chilly, brisk wind blew through the town. It's now or never, he thought. He tightened his grip and made his move. Up came the rifle, steadied as best he could through the searing pain of his crippled hand. He squeezed the trigger. CLICK! The hammer fell without effect. *Misfire!* He stood stone still, frozen in place, the rifle still aimed directly at its target, the distant crowd unaware of what had happened.

In that split second, Bedloe grabbed for his Colt. *He* knew instinctively he had the sheriff, it was all but over. One down, one to go. Mentally he was already packing his meager belongings in his tattered carpet bag, heading toward New Mexico and a chance to be somebody. He thumbed back the hammer as it cleared the holster, and, finger on the trigger, quickly raised it to fire on a man who stood without any further options, facing him in the street on that cold morning in Lake City, Colorado. A small dust devil swirled briefly off to one side, then —

CRAACK!

The sharp sound of the rifle broke the hushed silence like a bolt of lightning. The impact lifted Bedloe off his feet, dropping him back to the ground like a sack of potatoes. He lay motionless, spread-eagled on his back, the Colt still in his hand; one shot had discharged harmlessly into the dirt at his feet as he fell, an unconscious reaction when the rifle bullet slammed into him.

Tauber, nearly in shock, walked slowly to the unmoving body. As he stood over Bedloe, he stared in amazement at the gaping hole, a perfect shot, dead center in the middle of the forehead; a thin trail of blood trickled from the ugly wound. He stood painfully, mentally reexamining what had just happened, questioning how his rifle could have gone off after misfiring without his even realizing it, making a one-in-a-million shot. It was all just a blur. Then, he looked down at the rifle, struggled with the lever to pull the chamber open with his left hand, and as it moved slowly back, he knew. It was suddenly clear, crystal clear.

The crowd rushed into the street, shouting support for Tauber, for his ridding the town of a menace. They parted as the big sorrel approached. In the saddle, Jeremiah leaned over slightly to look into the face of the fallen man. He grunted, then looked at Tauber. The sheriff's eyes spoke volumes.

"Thanks, I'll never forget this. You can count on that," Tauber said as he looked up at the big man.

Jeremiah could see the depth of Tauber's gratitude in the relief on the sheriff's face; even the pain of the broken hand seemed diminished. As he lifted the reins, Jeremiah nodded and touched the brim of his hat with two fingers in a salute. He gave the mare a gentle nudge in the ribs with his boot heels, easing his way through the gathering crowd.

He took the road that would lead home, back to the peace and simplicity of the high mountains, where danger was simple, basic, never devious or calculating. He felt no remorse for the death of Creeg Bedloe. What he'd had to do that day took on a different significance than any before. This time he had encountered the enemy, knew who and what he was dealing with, and had seen the bad. And he knew the value in the man whose life he'd saved too. His deadly shot from the deep early morning shadows of an alley had not seemed a return to the horror-filled days of the war. The guilt was gone. He felt at peace with himself.

The trip to Lake City had not been just another uncounted journey to oblivion in a bar, steeped in remorse and self-recrimination. Instead, an opportunity to reexamine his own self-worth had been presented to him. He saw for the first time in many years a man he could live with after all. And it felt good. He breathed deeply of the clear air, as he spurred the mare on, and rode slowly out of town.

Somebody said, "Better let the doc up in Powderhorn look at that hand of your'n, Sheriff."

"Here, let me help you," said another.

Two men dragged Bedloe's body from the middle of the street to the walk in front of the barber shop, there to be tied to a wide pine board, propped against a porch post and displayed for public viewing for a respectable time, or at least until the flies got too bad. Trussed up and on exhibit, the corpse would be a fitting warning to others who would follow the same path. Creeg Bedloe would now be noticed by the whole community, even by strangers just riding through. And for the first time in his short life, he *would* be a somebody.

After the crowd disappeared, after the body had been taken away, after the sheriff was sitting at a table in the saloon being served free whiskey by an admiring crowd, the only thing left to let passersby know something had happened there that day, still lay in the middle of the street. There, half buried in the dirt from the shuffling of dozens of boots, was the Colt Peacemaker with the fancy carved grip and five bullets still in the chamber. Seventeen-year-old Johnny Beaver spotted it as he crossed the street. He stooped over to pick it up, tucked it in his belt, and quickly covered it with his shirttail. He glanced around to see if anyone had noticed, and, seeing no one, hurried straight to the livery, and the tiny room in the back where he lived.

CHAPTER SEVEN

Johnny Beaver had been orphaned since he was eight, left to make his own way on the hostile frontier by a Ute raiding party. His father had married a Shawnee Indian woman shortly after arriving in Kansas to work for the railroad, and Jonathan Truesdale, Jr. was born two years later. After his father was killed in a rail accident, his mother had no means of support, so, she indentured herself and young Johnny to a family planning to move to Colorado and open a dry goods store in Lake City.

In a mountain pass just east of their destination, the three wagons, full of furniture and fixtures, were ambushed by a band of Utes, killing every one of the eleven settlers except Johnny, who scampered unseen to the safety of the thick underbrush alongside the trail. The settlers had failed to hire a wagon master experienced in dealing with confrontations with Indians, and, without veteran leadership or direction, they succumbed quickly to the hail of arrows and gunfire that turned the slow moving group into panic-stricken victims.

The savages had approached from the heavy woods above the trail, well spread out. They had slowly and cautiously surrounded the three lumbering wagons, quickly sized up the risk and, seeing little potential resistance, proceeded to massacre what they thought to be everyone.

Oren Spicey, the store owner and self-appointed leader of the train, caught the first arrow. Completely surprised by the sudden attack, he looked down with innocent bewilderment at the wooden shaft that abruptly appeared, painfully erupting from his chest. He slowly slipped sideways out of the saddle onto the ground, dead before he hit the dirt.

When the shooting and whooping started, the team, pulling the wagon on which Johnny and his mother rode, bolted. The panicked driver struggled to control the team during the melee, but, startled as the gunfire erupted, the four mules jumped sharply at right angles to the heavily laden wagon, overturning it and pinning Johnny's mother beneath a wheel. Johnny was thrown clear, but his mother died instantly in the fall. Though she passed away leaving a young boy to fend for himself, her death was a blessing, as captive women received savage treatment from the Utes, serving as little more than pack animals and objects of derision and torture. She had, however, imbued young Johnny with a wealth of knowledge from her Shawnee heritage. Firmly implanted in his memory were survival skills that would serve him well the rest of his life. He had become an expert at secreting himself from others, able to lie stone quiet for hours, even controlling his breathing so as to make movement undetectable. When playing hide and seek with other children, he'd always win. This time it was for his life.

The Indians had scoured the wagons for cloth, trinkets, food and weapons, then, finding little need of furniture or wagons, set everything ablaze and rode off amidst bloodcurdling yells of victory.

Two days later, Johnny was found wandering further down the sometimes trail by gold miners on their way to Lake City to stake their claim. They had come upon the remains of the wagons, hastily buried the mutilated bodies, then continued cautiously on toward Lake City. When they found Johnny, they were surprised that anyone could have survived. They took the dazed and hungry boy on to town with them, leaving him in the care of the sheriff after reporting what they had discovered.

Sheriff Tauber had convinced the owner of the livery stable, Simon Stover, that the young boy could be a valuable asset working for him. Stover was at first reluctant. He didn't like the idea of housing the half-breed youth under his own roof. Never having been married, he'd not had much use for children, but after seeing how well Johnny took to animals, he decided to let him stay. He gave him room and board and a few coins in exchange for help in cleaning out the stalls, feeding and brushing down the horses, as well as any other odd job he could create. And he could create plenty. Crusty and rough, old man Stover slowly found himself becoming fond of having the boy around to talk to, though he was loathe to admit to having any such human trait. It was Simon who had changed the boy's name from Jonathan Truesdale. He gave him the name Johnny Beaver, both to keep the other boys from laughing at him because of his highfalutin' name and because the toothless old man never could pronounce Truesdale. Besides, Johnny Beaver had sort of an Indian ring to it. That seemed appropriate.

Nine years after Johnny came to Lake City, as the boy was reaching manhood, Simon began to feel he was losing touch with him, that there was some great longing hidden from sight, but growing. He generally brushed it off, assuming it had something to do with his Indian blood. It was there, sure enough, though it had nothing to do with his being half Shawnee. It had more to do with every young man's desire to prove himself, and be free of adult authority.

The night of Creeg Bedloe's death, Johnny waited until Simon was asleep, then went to where he had hidden the Colt beneath a stack of empty burlap bags. He carefully cleaned it of every speck of the dirt and mud from the street, then oiled and polished with fascination this beautiful instrument of death. Johnny felt a tinge of exhilaration as he handled the weapon by which two men had died. He held it close to the dim light of the oil lamp and rubbed its smooth finish like he was rubbing fine silver. He fingered the finely carved grips, then grasped it like a gunfighter testing for proper balance. It was the first time he had ever held a gun. It felt natural, exciting. The gun was special, almost magical, in the spell it cast over the impressionable young boy.

"This is my chance to truly make my own way," he muttered to the darkness. Then, rewrapping the Colt in one of the bags, he slipped it back under the stack in the darkest corner of the grain room. To really get somewhere, a person needed a gun, he reasoned, and fate had presented him with this magnificent gift — an opportunity was at hand. All he needed was a holster and belt, and some bullets, although there were five still in the cylinder when he picked it up. He would have to ask Mr. Stover for an advance on his wages. He could then go into the hills far from town and learn how to use his prized find.

"An advance on yer wages? Why boy, you'd just go spend it all, then what would ya do? Besides, what's a boy need with money when he's got food aplenty, proper clothes and a warm bed to sleep in?" Stover snorted and turned from Johnny to take the reins of a chestnut mare that needed brushing. He handed the reins to Johnny and started to leave.

"I just need a little money, that's all, Mr. Stover. Couldn't you see yer way to let me have just a little?" Johnny pleaded.

"Takes every cent I got just to run this

place, what with havin' to feed and house an extra hand. Sorry, son, I just ain't got none to spare." Stover pushed open the large, creaky doors at the front of the stable, then bent down to place two large rocks he kept nearby to hold them open.

Johnny knew times were tough. He understood. But, that didn't make it any easier to accept for a boy seeking his independence . . . and needing to buy bullets.

The autumn wind wafted through the drafty building. Johnny stood dejectedly, watching as Simon started up the street toward the saloon for his morning eye-opener. Half-heartedly, Johnny pulled a pig bristle brush from the top rail of a stall and began to brush down the mare. His mind drifted off to places he could only imagine as he stroked the horse's back, and pondered ways to get the money he needed. From somewhere in his head, a voice said, *Be patient.* But being patient and being seventeen weren't things that went together well.

CHAPTER EIGHT

James Duckworth stirred about in his room at the Gold Claim Hotel in the early morning. He washed his face in the fancy gilt-edged basin that sat on a small wash stand next to the bed, then buried his face in a thick, scratchy towel that hung above the stand on a peg. Lace curtains, worn and dusty, fluttered lazily from the chilly draft that snaked in around ill-fitting windows. He pulled a small bottle from his leather traveling case, opened it, then shook some rose water in his palm and ran his fingers through his hair, smiling with great satisfaction at what he saw in the mirror.

A slight man, in his late fifties, Duckworth prided himself on keeping fit and eating right, drinking in moderation, smoking only an occasional cigar, and tending strictly to business. He stayed away from the ladies as they would only serve to subvert his attention — not to mention his funds — from his financial interests. His thinning gray hair, oval glasses perched halfway down on a thin, straight nose, and walking cane with a silver handle made him look every inch the banker he was.

He had intended to be downstairs for an early breakfast as he had arranged to rent a buckboard from the livery to take him up to the Gold Doubloon mine. It was to be ready to go at eight, sharp.

Mr. Duckworth was an investor in various copper and silver mines, and had never even *seen* a gold mine. His interest in the Gold Doubloon prompted him to come all the way out from St. Louis to see the actual operation, because this mine was his only investment that had *never* turned one dime in profit for him. In fact, the man Duckworth had put in charge, Ezra Goode, had recently written and asked for additional funds, citing increasing costs for labor and supplies. Mr. Duckworth was less than convinced that Ezra Goode was the right man for the job, and had gone so far as to tell him so in a letter to Goode. Soon, he thought, he'd be on the scene to see for himself just what the situation really was.

He stood at the window, briefly staring out over the wide valley. In the distance, he thought he could see the snow-covered Uncompahgre Peak towering over lower mountains to the west. The sun's arrival had set its mantle ablaze with a bright yellow glow. He was taken with the serene beauty of the mountains, but even he, a flatlander, could tell from the splashes of glistening gold of the aspen trees dotting the hills that yet another harsh winter was rapidly approaching, and he thanked God he was a businessman instead of a miner. The very thought of having to endure winters where the snow drifted higher than many houses back home, gave him swift reason to want to finish his business as quickly as possible and head back East before any chance of an early blizzard caught him and held him there for the duration.

He thought about why he was there and about the men who seemed irresistibly drawn to those majestic mountains, risking everything to seek unknown fortunes. It was the thought of those unknown fortunes that jarred him back to the task at hand and away from the picturesque scene out his hotel window. He closed and locked the door behind him as he started down the long, narrow hall toward the stairway, and breakfast.

The stiff-springed seat of the buckboard

seemed to Duckworth to be jarring loose every tooth in his head on the trip out to the Gold Doubloon mine, and he thought perhaps he would have been better advised to ride a horse. But, horses never seemed to take a liking to him. So, from the time as a youth he'd been thrown from the back of a supposedly mild-mannered bay mare back in St. Louis, he kept a respectable distance between himself and horses. The only exception was his cautious willingness to ride well behind them in any of several different types of conveyances that kept him from having to walk.

A barely discernible trail led from town into the hills where evidence of numerous placer claims could be found situated near several streams that ambled down from the surrounding peaks. He had followed that route for about two hours when he came upon a small operation some miles from Lake City. He reined in the horse near where some prospectors were gathered around a sluice. As he sat holding the reins, he called to them.

"I beg your pardon, gentlemen, but could one of you direct me to the Gold Doubloon mine?"

A fat, slovenly man strolled over to the buckboard, giving Duckworth a squinty-eyed stare, as he pushed back his moth-eaten, eastern-style, derby hat. He wiped dirty sweat from his brow on the sleeve of his long johns. A cotton shirt was wrapped around his waist and tied in front with the sleeves. "What d'ya want with the Gold Doubloon?" he asked.

"I'm the owner, and I wish to seek out the mine foreman, Mr. Goode," Duckworth said.

The miner snorted and turned to the others. "Hear that? This fella come to *seek out* ol' Goode," the miner called back, then turned to Duckworth as the entire group of ragtag miners laughed uproariously.

"I really fail to see the humor in that," Duckworth said stiffly.

"You'd see the humor if you was to expect to find that ol' fool out here where the work's bein' done," the miner sneered.

"I . . . I don't understand. I'm sure he'll be at the mine, at this time of day, with all the other men I employ."

"Hell, mister, there ain't no other men. That worthless hole was played out years ago. An' besides, minin' turned out to be more work than ol' Ezra was up to." The prospector gave a single wave of his hand and started back down the path to rejoin the others, then stopped, and looked over his shoulder. "But if you just have to see fer yourself, what's left of the mine is up the trail about a quarter mile, on the right. Probably still a sign tacked to the entrance. Watch yerself, though, they's a heap of loose boulders that can easy come crashin' down on a man if he ain't takin' care."

"Much obliged," Duckworth said, frowning. He clicked his tongue and slapped the horse's rump with the reins to spur him on.

Very late that afternoon, when his chores were finished for the day, Johnny Beaver decided to take a walk to the edge of town to be alone. He often went to a certain spot on an outcropping of rocks where he could sit and watch the swirling river wend its way through the rugged terrain. As he watched a hawk, soaring in endless circles above the ridge, he noticed he could see his breath in the cool, early evening air, something he hadn't seen for months.

The days are getting shorter and if I'm to become independent and move south where the opportunities are, he thought, I'm going to have to find some money before winter sets in and I'm stuck here 'til spring. He'd heard that Santa Fe had opportunities for enterprising young men. He decided that's where he'd go. But, first, he needed money

75

for a ticket on the stage, and, of course, for a holster and bullets, for without a gun strapped to his belt, he wouldn't be really independent at all. In fact, he'd be just another runaway boy — running to what, he certainly didn't know. But he had this urge, and the simple act of holding the gleaming Colt in his hand gave him the courage to strike out on his own.

Returning to town at dusk, he passed the saloon where miners were rushing in to get the best place at the bar, or even better, one of the faro tables. Simon didn't allow the boy in the saloon, so Johnny didn't really know what faro was. But, it sounded exciting. He'd heard many a man say he was headed to the Nugget to "buck the tiger." He was thinking of this as he hurried along, not watching where he was going. He ran smack into Ezra Goode, nearly knocking the man off his feet.

"Watch where you're headed, you damned breed," Ezra growled.

"I'm real sorry, Mr. Goode. Guess I wasn't payin' proper attention. I'm sorry," Johnny said, nervously backing away as he pulled off his floppy hat and crumpled it to his chest.

"Where the hell you goin' in such an all-fired hurry?" Ezra grabbed the boy by his shirt sleeve to keep him from moving on.

"Got to do the evening feedin' and I'm . . . I'm late. I stayed too long up on the ridge." Johnny strained unsuccessfully to break the tough old miner's grip.

"What was you doin' up there, anyhow?"

"Jus thinkin', that's all. I sometimes go up there to do my thinkin'." With anxiety in his voice, Johnny finally pulled loose from the man's gnarled hand and rubbed his arm to straighten the wrinkles from his sleeve.

"And what's a young half-breed got to think about that's so damned important?" Ezra edged toward Johnny as the boy tried to move backwards away from him. "What wuz you thinkin' about this time?" This time, Ezra grasped Johnny's thin wrist and held him with an iron grip. Johnny struggled but could not free himself this time.

"About . . . about money . . . where I could get some . . . strike out on my own," he blurted out as he pulled and twisted. The old man just held on tighter.

"What's the likes of you need money fer?" Ezra asked.

"For . . . in case I should take a mind to travel . . . or somethin'."

"You? Travel? Ha! Travelin's fer proper folks, no stinkin' breed."

"I didn't say I *was* goin' nowhere. The

money's for just in case," Johnny said, scowling at the crusty miner's slanderous words.

"Make you a deal," the grizzled old man sneered and squinted one eye, contorting his dark, wrinkled face, "I'll give you some money . . . fer that knife you got there on yer belt." He reached down for the shiny, black hilt of the knife that hung at Johnny's side.

"No! I . . . I jus' couldn't. It was my pa's, and it isn't right to sell the only thing a person has to remind him of his pa who's dead and gone." Johnny could see an evil gleam in Ezra's eyes and his fear made him struggle that much harder. He kicked at the leg of his attacker, nearly losing his own balance.

Out of the shadows by the alley between the saloon and Lawyer Canada's Assay Office stepped Simon Stover, who had watched the struggle. "Let the boy go, Ezra," he said in a stern, cool voice. "Go on, boy, get to yer evenin' chores. Git!"

Ezra released his grip and grinned widely, showing gaps where teeth used to be.

"Don't go gettin' so all fired crotchety, Simon. Just havin' some fun with the little redskin, that's all." Ezra stood up to his full height, putting one hand on the butt of his rusty old Colt Navy model .44 to show his willingness to defend himself if it became necessary. It didn't, as Simon simply turned and walked away, following Johnny into the livery. Ezra gave a hearty laugh, brushed off his pants leg where Johnny had kicked dirt on him, and entered the smoke-filled saloon for his evening's entertainment.

As Johnny walked, the voice in his head said, *You were right not to sell your heritage.* About that, Johnny felt good.

It was after dusk when James Duckworth pulled up in front of the livery to return the buckboard. He was tired, dusty, and damned angry. What the old prospector had claimed, had proven to be true. The Gold Doubloon hadn't been worked for months, and, as far as he could tell, there was no sign of other workers having ever been there. It appeared he'd been sending money all this time to a man who was keeping it for himself, without ever swinging a pick or turning a shovel.

After returning the team to Simon Stover at the livery, Duckworth went straight to the sheriff's office to file a complaint. As he pushed open the creaky door and stepped into the light, he found Sheriff John C. Tauber at his desk, poring over a stack of papers. Tauber looked up as Duckworth entered, taking one more sip of steaming, day-old coffee from a tin cup.

"What can I do for you?" the sheriff asked.

"Sir, I should be obliged to file a complaint against one of your locals," Duckworth said, brushing the trail dust from his herring-bone suit with his hat.

"And who might that citizen be?"

"A Mr. Ezra Goode, the foreman of the Gold Doubloon mine."

"Pull up a chair mister. Uh, I didn't catch the name," Tauber said. He was rubbing his hand — the one Creeg Bedloe crushed that night in the alley — which had healed properly, but seemed to stiffen up on him during the cool, humid evenings. He swung around and reached into one of the cubicles in the roll-top desk along the wall for a piece of paper, opened the silver cap on a heavy glass inkwell and dipped a pen in the black ink.

"Duckworth, James Duckworth, investment banker from St. Louis, and owner of the Gold Doubloon mine."

Sheriff Tauber began slowly scratching the information Duckworth gave him on the sheet of paper. "And just what has ol' Ezra done this time, Mr. Duckworth?"

"Theft, my good man. It seems evident

that Mr. Goode has been taking money from me under false pretenses for over a year. I came out here to find why the mine had not returned one red cent in profit in over three years, and I discovered that Mr. Goode hadn't even been working the mine, simply pocketing the funds I've sent him for operating expenses and payroll." Duckworth leaned forward in the creaky wooden chair, his forehead wrinkled with anger and his face red with embarrassment for having been so easily duped.

The sheriff scratched several more words on the paper, then blotted them with a half-moon blotter. He sat back in his chair as he finished, pushing the paper toward Duckworth. "If you'll sign this complaint, I'll get Judge Barnes to fill out a warrant first thing in the morning. Then I'll bring Mr. Goode in. However, I expect he's spent all your money by now. There probably won't be much left to salvage, if I know Ezra. He's always been no more'n a lazy, good for nothin' troublemaker."

"Thank you, Sheriff, I'm most interested in seeing the scoundrel get his come-uppance. I shall await word from you of his incarceration. I'm staying at the Gold Claim, just down the street, room twenty." Duckworth rose and started for the door.

As he was leaving, he noticed a dozen or more wanted posters tacked to the wall next to the window. *Ezra Goode should be on one of those,* he thought.

CHAPTER NINE

Johnny immediately set to feeding the four horses that were housed at the livery for that night. He went to the feed room and dragged two burlap bags of oats across the dirt floor to the stalls. As he tugged at his bulky load, he glanced over at the stack of empty bags and thought of the prize he had hidden beneath them. He suddenly saw himself handling the situation with Ezra in a totally different way. That old miner would have thought twice before manhandling him if he'd had the Peacemaker strapped to his side instead of hidden in a burlap bag. Someone else would have had to crawl away with his tail between his legs — or worse.

He heard the creaking of the doors and he knew Simon had come in behind him. He was quickly brought back to reality and knew he had to get on with his job. But, he wouldn't always have to feed and clean up after horses, he thought, someday soon he'd have a future. He wasn't just some ignorant half-breed, he could read and write and even do ciphering. And he was in possession of a magnificent weapon, one that would make men keep their distance.

"Best just stay away from that one, boy; he's mean. Natural mean. I once saw him shoot a mongrel dog simply because he was sittin' in the middle of the road," Simon said. As he walked past Johnny, he reached out to pat the boy on the shoulder.

"Yes sir, I'll remember that. Thanks." Johnny smiled at the gesture. He was darned happy that Simon had arrived when he did, since there was no telling where things might have progressed.

With long, nearly pitch-black hair, and flashing black eyes, Johnny was tall and skinny, with a thin, bronzed face and hollow cheekbones. Handsome, some would say, if, that is, they could get past the fact that he was half Indian. Back in Kansas, he'd been accepted by most everyone, but, in Colorado, where men were being killed every day by roving bands of Ute, Arapaho and Cheyenne warriors, he was just one step from being one of the enemy.

Johnny was quiet, intelligent and quick to learn. The little voice in his head had told him early on that the best way to make his way was to keep to himself and observe others. He listened to the voice and caught on fast. Even those who didn't care for the color of his skin, had to admit that his easygoing manner and quiet demeanor were attributes they wished were displayed by more of their own children.

As he drew the brush across the back of a roan mare, his thoughts turned to what Ezra had said, the offer he had made. He cursed under his breath. The knife he carried at his side was the only possession he escaped with after the massacre besides the clothes on his back. It was a very old, short dagger — a dirk his father had called it — in a black leather scabbard with metal studs outlining the edges. Johnny's grandfather brought it with him when he came from England. It had been passed on from father to son for generations.

Johnny stopped brushing and pulled the knife from its sheath. It was still shiny and the black ebony handle was smooth with a soft, velvety feel. The blade came nearly straight down to a point, without much curve. It flashed in the light of the lamp as he turned it. He wondered if it had ever been used to kill anyone, then he remembered once when he was only four or five, his father had told him never to take it from its resting place in anger, unless he was prepared to use it for its intended purpose. And he sensed it *had* seen that purpose. Johnny knew he could never sell it, no matter what the need or reason. He would have to find another way to get the money he needed.

He was still staring at the shiny blade of the knife when Simon walked up to the stall next to the one Johnny was in and threw a saddle and blanket over the top rung.

"Sheriff Tauber would like you to clean up his saddle when you finish with the horses," Simon said as he pulled a dark cheroot from his shirt pocket and struck a match across a rough plank at the end of the stall. He took a long, satisfying draw of smoke into his mouth, then slowly, sporadically, pushed it out, making little rings of smoke that drifted lazily toward a peg that held a bridle.

"I'll be finished in a bit, sir," Johnny answered.

"Fine. I'll be turnin' in early, then. Fer some reason I seem to be intolerably weary, tonight." Simon yawned and strode across the barn to his room at the front, near the double doors.

Johnny slept in the back, next to the grain room, in a small space he shared with tools and many large pieces of leather to be used to repair harnesses. The room was dry, though drafty, a fact he didn't really mind, since he figured that the occasional drafts were the only source of fresh air he got while being cooped up with the pungent odor of all that rawhide.

As he finished with the last horse, Johnny heard Simon open the little metal box that held the livery's receipts. He could hear coins being dropped into it, some of them muffled by the stack of paper money he kept in there too. Simon had never trusted the bank, harboring a special dislike for the banker, Avril Goodman, a man he felt lived off the hard earned gains of others. "You'll never catch me givin' that man one red cent to squander on his fancy women," Simon had been heard to declare on more than one occasion.

Ezra Goode leaned over one of the faro tables at the Little Nugget Saloon, staking his last few dollars on a change of luck. He let out an oath as his "sure thing bet" once again soured and his last dollar went to the dealer. He pushed his way through the crowd that had gathered to watch and drink, stopping at the end of the bar to check his pockets, making certain he was indeed completely broke.

"Looks like you oughta give up gamblin', Ezra," said a fat, unshaven man leaning on the bar.

"Mind yer own business," Ezra shot back, then turned to the bartender. "How about one fer the road, on the house?"

"You know the policy, Ezra, no free drinks. You better jus' go home and forget tonight," the bartender said, as he leaned against the back bar, wiping a glass with his dirty towel.

"Aww, to hell with yer rules," Ezra said through gritted teeth. He slapped his hand on the bar, then pushed away and started for the door, just as one of his cronies rushed up to him.

"Ezra, I've got to talk to you. Let's go outside," puffed a scrawny, toothless, dirty little man with a beard, limping from a long forgotten accident in a long forgotten mine. He was tugging impatiently at Ezra's sleeve as the two slipped through the doors and into the dark alley next to the saloon.

"What the hell's this all about, Benson?" Ezra said as he pulled away from the man's grip on his sleeve.

"There's a man in town that wants you arrested. And the sheriff's gonna do it, just as soon as Judge Barnes signs the warrant tomorrow. You best git outta here," the man said, short of breath and wheezing.

"Now, where in the hell did you get information like that, Benson? Tell me, how?"

"I was in the alley, outside the jail when I overheard the sheriff through the open window, so I know it as bein' true."

"What was this man's name?"

"Uh, Duck somethin' or other."

"Duckworth?" Ezra's face grew pale with the news.

"Yeh, that's it, Duckworth. You know him?"

"Yeh . . . thanks, Benson," Ezra said, as a scowl came over his face. He pushed the little man aside, and rushed into the street towards the hotel. He knew that if James Duckworth was in town, his goose was cooked.

As he approached the Gold Claim Hotel, he stopped on the porch to peer in through the lace curtains at the large front window. The desk clerk was not at the desk as Ezra quietly opened the door and tiptoed across the dimly lit room to the desk register. There, written on the left-hand page, was the name of the man who, at this moment, he feared more than anyone: James Duckworth, room twenty. He retraced his steps and slipped out the front door, then hurried around the two-story building to the back stairway. His aim was to talk some sense into Duckworth. He didn't want to go to jail. As he eased his way down the hall, he spotted Duckworth's room and tapped lightly on the door.

"Just a minute," Duckworth called out. Then, seconds later, he opened the door. "Yes?"

"I need to speak to you, Mr. Duckworth," Ezra said.

"Who are you?" Duckworth asked.

Ezra pushed firmly on the door as Duckworth stepped back. Once inside, he closed the door behind himself and said, "The name's Ezra Goode."

Duckworth's eyes opened wide and his face flushed from the anger he felt at the man who stood before him. "I have nothing to say to you, I trusted you and you stole from me. You'll pay for that dishonor. Now, get out of here!"

Ezra took a step toward Duckworth, who clenched his fists in resentment that the man would have the brazenness to push his way into his hotel room and confront him.

Ezra put his hand on Duckworth's shoulder to calm him down, but the banker from St. Louis would have none of it as he slapped Ezra's hand away.

"Look, I just wanta talk, work this thing out. There's gold in that mine, honest. I had a run of bad luck, that's all," Ezra pleaded.

"You're through robbing me! And, you'll be under arrest come morning. Now, leave my room, immediately!" Duckworth put his hand in the middle of Ezra's chest and shoved him back into the door. Ezra's hand went immediately for the .44 that hung in a holster at his side, he drew it and jammed the barrel in Duckworth's stomach. As he pulled the old Colt, he instinctively pulled the hammer back to the firing position. He was trapped and he knew it; they would arrest him in the morning and the evidence was insurmountable. He knew he would be going to prison, and the man who would send him there was unwilling to even talk about it, reason it out, or give him another chance.

Ezra knew he'd probably be sent to Yuma. That thought alone made him shudder. He'd heard all the stories about how many men die there, and there was no doubt in his mind that he couldn't take the punishment from guards with a reputation for harsh brutality. There was no other choice. He fired the gun, point blank into a defenseless James Duckworth, whose body was slammed back against the wall. Duckworth stared blankly at his attacker, unwilling to believe that even this unscrupulous man would stoop to murder. Then, as darkness overcame his senses, he slipped to the floor, dead.

In a panic, Ezra slammed the door behind him as he rushed from the room and down the back stairs. Into the black night, he ran.

CHAPTER TEN

The task of brushing and feeding completed, Johnny carried the empty feed bags to the grain room, then returned with a bucket of water and some saddle soap. He pulled the sheriff's saddle off its perch and dumped it in the middle of the floor near the only oil lamp still wicked up, and plopped down on a small, three-legged stool beside it. He was, himself, weary from the long day and he nodded off several times as he tried to concentrate on cleaning and polishing the well-worn saddle.

In fact, it was during one of his lapses into temporary sleep that a figure eased from the dark shadows and silently came toward him from behind. Something, some sixth sense perhaps, shook him out of his daze just before a splintering blow to the head sent him sprawling, across the saddle, face down on the straw on the floor. He heard no sound as he fell other than a slight shuffle of straw as he made a feeble attempt at moving his hand, then, he descended into a swirling blackness.

When he awoke in the middle of the night, he thought his head would burst from the throbbing. He couldn't make his eyes focus and, as he reached up to brush some straw from his hair, he drew his hand back as he felt something wet, sticky. The flickering light from the oil lamp revealed a hand covered with blood — his blood.

For several minutes, he just lay there, across the saddle where he had fallen. He tried to recollect what had happened, but all he could remember was searing pain, and that was clearly implanted in the present as well as the past. He tried to push himself up on one elbow, but fell back again as a sharp, blinding pain shot from the back of his skull, over the top of his head, and centered in his right eye. Drying blood matted his hair in back and a thin trail of brownish red trailed down his cheek. He lay, unmoving, breathing in agonizing, short gasps. "Mr. Stover . . . Mr. Stover . . . ," he groaned, then lapsed into unconsciousness once again.

It was not yet dawn when he awoke for the second time, finally able to lift himself to a sitting position, though dizzy and unsteady. He reached out for the bridle that hung above him on a peg, grasped it and pulled himself to his feet. His legs were shaky, and he dragged his feet as he made his way to the door of Simon's room. He pounded on it.

"Mr. Stover . . . I'm hurt," he murmured as he leaned against the rough-sawn wood of the doorway. "Sir . . . ," he called again. But just then, his weight proved too much for the flimsy latch and the door gave way, sending him stumbling inside. A hazy moon cast a dim shaft of light through the window to illuminate the small room. Then, as he shook his head and waved his arms about to clear the air of the dust from his indelicate entrance, he saw Simon Stover sprawled out on the floor, near his bed, face down with a knife in his back. Not just any knife, either. The shiny black ebony handle unmistakably identified the cruel weapon as Johnny's.

Unconsciously, Johnny's hand shot to his belt, not fully believing his eyes, hoping against hope that his knife would still be there, nestled firmly in its sheath where it had always been. But it was not to be and he recoiled with fear at the sight of the old man laying in a pool of blood, motionless. Johnny crawled to the still body and shook him. He pulled back quickly when he saw the old man's eyes, open, staring into the dirt, empty and dead.

Johnny scrambled to get out of the room. He fell over a bale of hay and just lay there for several minutes, trying to make some sense of what had happened, then he reached out, shaking, to take the knife, his knife, from Simon's back. At the touch, he was overcome by a wave of fear. He recoiled, scooting back to lean against the crude wooden frame that served as a bed. He couldn't do it. The knife would have to stay.

His whole body throbbed with pain. He put his head down across his arm on the straw-filled mattress; tears filled his eyes. *What am I going to do? What will happen to me now?* He decided he'd better go tell the sheriff. Then, a sudden rush of apprehension swept over him when he noticed the tin money box overturned on the floor beside him. Empty. *What if the sheriff thinks I did it? They'll all think I did it.* Who'd take the word of a half-breed kid, anyway? His thoughts were a torrent of mixed emotions: Fear, sadness, confusion, pain.

Then he remembered the Colt, tucked away under the empty feed sacks. He'd get the gun, hold it. It might give him a better perspective, a better feel for what to do.

First, however, he needed to wash up.

He made his way slowly through the darkness to the back of the barn to wash his wound in the watering trough. Every step sent a stabbing pain through his head. He took the small jar of water that sat on the shelf above the trough, poured it into the head of the pump to prime it, then drew the long wooden handle up and down several times until fresh, cool water began to gush out. He dutifully refilled the priming jar and placed it back where he'd found it, then continued slowly to pump as he stuck his head under the flow of water, letting the soothing flow ease the hurt and the throbbing. After cleaning himself up, he reached for the towel that hung from a peg next to the shelf and buried his face in it. Once dry, he replaced the towel on the peg, giving no thought to the fact that Simon would no longer be aware of his neatness, nor would he ever again praise him for it.

His heart was pounding as a wild assemblage of thoughts darted about in his head: Who could have done this awful thing? What should he do now? Should he go to the sheriff? No. No, he was sure no one would believe it wasn't him that killed Simon, since it was his knife that was used. They'd think he did it for the money. He'd told several people in the last few days he needed money and he was going to ask Simon for it. Why hadn't he just kept it to himself? Damn. He could run, but to where? South, maybe, to New Mexico or Arizona. Yes, south. It would be a while before anyone found the body and by then he could be several miles away. He'd have to have a horse, however, since he didn't own one himself. He could take one of Simon's. After all, Simon wouldn't be needing a horse anymore and he was sure the old man would want it that way. Yes, the gray gelding, a good rimrocker, that's the one he'd take, along with a saddle, that old one in the grain room that Simon wanted to sell but never found a buyer for. Too beat up from some cowboy's rough treatment everyone said. It ain't worth the price. It would serve Johnny just fine.

Johnny gathered up his bedroll, rolled it tightly and tied it with strips of rawhide. He shoved some hardtack, dried beans, and a small bag of flour into a saddlebag, then filled a canteen with water. He hurriedly wadded up his meager belongings and clothing, stuffing them in the other saddlebag. The last item, and the most important, was the shiny Colt revolver, which he drew from the gunny sack and shoved into his belt. Once the gray was saddled and ready, Johnny led him out the back door into the alley, then mounted and walked him slowly south toward the lake. As he left, he noticed that one of the other horses was missing: Mr. Steven's bay mare. Probably wandered off through the open back door. Strange, he didn't remember leaving that door open before he settled in to work on the sheriff's saddle. Oh well, he couldn't worry about that now. Time was of the essence.

In minutes he was free of the town, a town he was sure would turn against him just as soon as they discovered the body of one of the town's best-loved citizens: Simon Stover.

The first glow of dawn began painting warm reds and yellows on the peaks to the west, and a light breeze sent shimmering ripples across the lake as he rode swiftly down the south road toward freedom. The smell of pine and juniper burning in cook-stoves — marking the start of early break-fasts in many of the cabins that dotted the hills above the scant trail along the water's edge — made him sad to be leaving the place that had been home to him for so many years. He stopped the gray for a mo-ment, and looked back toward the old barn, built of log beams and whipsaw siding, with a steep tin roof to shed the winter's heavy snows. He took a deep breath, and wondered if he'd made a mistake; after all, the townsfolk knew Johnny Beaver to be a gentle, kind, and hard-working young man. Maybe they should be given a chance to prove that they are fair-minded, not prone to jumping to hasty conclusions. But, what if? That nagging doubt drove him to spur the gray on, knowing that while the majority of Lake City's residents were honest, willing to give a man every chance to prove himself innocent, there were those few troublemakers that could sway a town eager to find someone to take the blame for a senseless death. And how could he prove himself innocent, anyway? The knife had been his. Everyone knew that. And the money was missing. More than a few people knew he wanted money — though, for what they didn't know — and that didn't look good for him. Not good at all.

It would make good reading in the *Silver World* newspaper that Harry Woods printed in his log cabin. Harry had made quite a stir the day he reported on Creeg Bedloe's death. He sold more papers that one day than he had in weeks. Johnny hated the thought that he might be tomorrow's headline.

"Come on fella," he said as he jammed

his bootheels in the big horse's ribs. "No time to waste lookin' back." He knew it was going to be a rugged trip, through high mountain passes already starting to gather early snow, and across treacherous gorges with raging rivers dropping from 14,000 foot-high Red Cloud Peak. He would follow the Lake Fork to its headwaters in the San Juans, then on to Eureka, Howardsville and Silverton, on the Animas River, then down to Durango. Once in Durango, he figured he could decide whether to continue south to New Mexico or turn southwest to Arizona.

CHAPTER ELEVEN

The night clerk at the Gold Claim had thought he heard a gunshot during the night, but, having heard them so many times in a town where drunks fired their weapons sometimes 'til dawn, he was unconcerned. It wasn't until Mr. Duckworth didn't come down to early breakfast as he had indicated he would, that the clerk went upstairs to room twenty to check on him. That's when, upon pushing open the unlocked door after getting no response to his knock, he found the body, propped against the wall. A trail of dried blood stained the flowered wallpaper.

James Duckworth's eyes were frozen open and his mouth twisted in painful surprise at his fate, his fists still tightly clenched from the anger he felt for the man he pushed too far. The clerk stepped back in horror at the sight. He covered his mouth with his hand as he turned to run from the room, sick to his stomach. He ran down the street toward the sheriff's office, yelling, "He's been murdered! He's been murdered!"

Sheriff Tauber stepped from the front door of the jail, pulling up his suspenders with one hand and buttoning his fly with the other. "What the hell's all the racket? Who's been murdered?"

"That banker from St. Louis. Mr. Duckworth," the clerk blurted out as he came to a sudden, dusty halt in front of the jail. Shaken badly by the sight of a dead man in his hotel, the clerk started sobbing. "There's blood everywhere, he's been SHOT!" He put a hand to his forehead and hung his head.

"Wait'll I get my shirt on. I'll be right there," Tauber said as he raced back inside.

Several people had gathered outside the room of the murdered man as the sheriff reached the top of the stairs. He pushed his way into the room, stopped, then gave a deep groan at the sight before him. He knelt down beside the body, then looked back at the door, crowded with the curious.

"Go on back to your rooms, there's nothin' here for you," he said as he waved them away. He motioned for the clerk to come in and said, "Matt, go find Macmillan and tell him we're goin' to need a posse. You come along, too, and, oh, go over to

103

the livery and get Simon to saddle my horse."

"You got any idea who done this, Sheriff?" Matt asked.

"Got an idea." Tauber frowned, then said, "Get goin', we're losin' time."

The clerk turned and ran down the stairs as Tauber closed the door to Duckworth's room. On his way to the jail, the sheriff made a brief stop at the undertaker's to place an order for a casket.

He had no sooner reached the other side of the street when Matt, the desk clerk, came screaming from the livery stable.

"It's Simon! My God, he's dead too! And Johnny's gone," he yelled, his arms flailing, nearly falling over his own feet in his distress.

Thomas Macmillan was just coming from the side door to the stone building that housed the volunteer fire department. He and Tauber met in the middle of the street, then ran side by side to the livery. Tauber drew his sidearm as he halted just outside the front doors. He held up his arm to signal others to stop and wait outside, then carefully slipped in between the partially opened doors. He stopped momentarily to let his eyes adjust to the near-dark interior, then proceeded cautiously toward Simon's room.

His eyes darted about, surveying the barn to be sure he was alone. He nearly stumbled over his own saddle, next to a hay bale in the middle of his path. Even in the dim early morning light, he could make out blood on the pommel. He bent down to examine it and noticed more blood on the straw covering the floor. He cocked the hammer of the .44, in case the killer was still inside, then eased his way into the small, drafty room where Simon lay, dead, face down next to his bed. The sheriff muttered something under his breath, then stood up and rushed out into the street. "Get a posse together, NOW!" he yelled to Macmillan. "Find six or seven who can ride."

"What happened to Simon?" Macmillan queried.

"Same thing that happened to that banker, he was murdered."

"I seen that black-handled knife stickin' out of Simon's back," Matt said angrily. "It was Johnny's. We all knew he was needin' money for some reason or 'nother. You think he killed the old man, Sheriff?"

"Hell, NO! Johnny couldn't kill a jackrabbit! Besides, if he done it, do you think he'd leave his own knife there as evidence against him?"

"Reckon not," Matt said, still shaken from

the two grisly discoveries.

"It was left there on purpose to make us think it was the boy."

"Then, what happened to Johnny?" Macmillan asked.

"Someone else was hurt in there too. Got a good idea it was Johnny. It looks like he was cleanin' my saddle when he got hit, hard! I'd say someone probably snuck up on him from behind. He may have been unconscious when the killin' occurred. Don't know where he's got to, though, or how bad he's hurt."

"Any idea who done it, then?" one of the men who'd gathered outside asked.

"Got a hunch it was Ezra Goode. Somehow, he musta found out there was goin' to be a warrant issued on him this mornin' and he went to settle things with that banker," Tauber answered.

"And, needin' a horse, and some cash, the livery musta seemed his best bet. He's probably headed south into the pass. I'll bet he's figuring we'll never find him if he gets through to Eureka. We'll pick up his trail easy enough if I'm right."

"What about Johnny? Where'd he go?"

"Tell the mayor to get some folks out lookin' around town for Johnny. He's probably hurt, wandering around somewhere.

I'll meet all of you in front of the jail in twenty minutes."

So far, the gently sloping foothills between the town and the San Juan Range to the south had proven easy going, and by the early afternoon, Johnny found himself getting hungry. He reined-in the gray at a stream crossing, dismounted to let the horse drink and graze on buffalo grass. Johnny climbed a small knoll to sit and rest, enjoy the soft warmth of the sun, and sample some of the jerky and hardtack he'd brought along. As he rested at the edge of a stand of yellow-leafed aspen, he thought he saw a dust cloud rising, off in the distance, coming from the direction of town. That couldn't be a posse, he thought. Or could it? Could they have picked up my trail already?

Taking no chances, he ran back down the knoll to where the gray stood, ears standing straight as if he, too, knew someone was approaching. Johnny shoved the jerky and hardtack back in the saddlebag, swung into the saddle and urged the gray toward a draw upstream. If he could get a little higher into the hills, he knew of a canyon whose floor was almost solid rock, making it much more difficult to track a rider. It would give him a chance to put added distance between himself and his pursuers. He leaned forward in the saddle, kicked the big horse hard in the ribs, spurring him to a spurt of speed toward the craggy spires of the San Juans straight ahead.

The rough terrain made the going difficult and he was not able to cover as much ground as he'd hoped. As the gray threaded its way among jagged boulders and scrub junipers, loose rocks and occasional shale breaks, Johnny noticed he'd cut the trail of another horse, traveling much the same route and direction as he'd chosen. The tracks appeared fresh, as though the horse and rider had passed through only a few hours earlier. Johnny reined-in the gray, dismounted and squatted down to get a better look at the prints. Deftly, he touched the damp soil where the horse's hooves had pressed deeply. He recognized the distinctive markings at once. The prints were those of the horse that had been taken from the livery: Mr. Steven's bay mare. The horse hadn't wandered off after all. She must have been stolen, most likely by Simon's killer, the same person that whacked Johnny over the head.

The ground had been ascending slowly toward the majestic peaks, and Johnny realized that he was between the posse and the probable killer. Soon, he would have to make a decision to either trail the killer himself or try to shake the posse. As he crested a rise, he saw a fresh dusting of snow, leading all the way to the hard rock canyon floor, making it impossible to continue in that direction and still avoid detection. Cutting through the pass was the shortest way over the mountains, but without benefit of cover, or clear, hard-packed terrain to give few clues as to his having passed that way, the obvious route would be to skirt the cliffs, paralleling, but staying below, the snow line, and pray he'd come upon a lower pass. It would take much longer that way, but he would be much harder to track. Still, the tracks of the bay led straight into the pass, through the snow, leaving an easy trail to follow.

He sat for a few moments, trying to decide his next move. He knew the posse was closing in, that they were only about an hour or so behind, and that if he was to turn away from the pass, they might just follow the more obvious tracks, affording him time to escape through some lower trail to the southwest. It was a good plan, but could he do it? For all his desire to get away from Lake City, to become someone on his own, could he abandon the opportunity to follow the bay's trail and find out for himself who the real killer was? Maybe he'd even bring in the murderin' thief and clear his own name. A big risk. At least, he had a gun, that wonderful Colt that Creeg Bedloe had ordered special, then lost in the dirt when he was shot down. But, could he use it when the chips were down?

He turned in the saddle and looked back. He could see no one, but he knew they were there, and coming fast. Freedom was a strong temptation and it was in his grasp. Could he just run, never knowing who murdered the man who'd been like a father to him for nine years? Simon Stover had taken him in, clothed and fed him when no one else wanted a half-breed living under his roof. He owed Simon for being the father he'd lost as a child. Johnny knew he really had no choice. He had to try no matter what the cost. He spurred the gray forward, heading directly into the snowy pass, following the tracks that would lead him toward whatever unknown lay ahead.

CHAPTER TWELVE

Sheriff John Tauber raised his hand and reined-in his horse. The six-man posse strung out behind slowed to a stop, then gathered around him. He sat for a moment, moving his head back and forth as he looked down at the tracks they'd been following.

"What's the matter, Sheriff? Why'd we stop?" one of the group asked. They were all just plain townsfolk, not real lawmen, and only a few understood tracking and signs. They certainly didn't understand why the sheriff suddenly decided to pull up when they thought they were making good time toward catching a killer.

"We've just cut another trail. Someone else has either joined him or is now also tracking him. Hard to say which right now," the sheriff said as he patted the neck of his black mare. He stood up in his stirrups and pulled his hat brim down low to shade his eyes from the sun, as he strained to see where the trail might logically lead. "My guess is someone else is tracking him. And I think I just figured out who."

"Who?" asked Matt Carver, the night desk clerk at the hotel.

"The third victim, the one I'd almost forgotten: Johnny Beaver."

"Yeah, you may be right. You figured Johnny'd been beat up pretty bad when you saw the blood on your saddle. And we didn't find him in town. Guess we never figured he'd go after Ezra fer killin' Simon," Matt said.

"I *should* have figured it that way when we saw two horses missin' from the livery. I reckon I was so mad about Simon, and that knife of Johnny's bein' used to throw blame on the boy, I forgot about Johnny bein' missin'. Damn! He's out there ahead of us, probably unarmed, hurt, and tryin' to corral a killer. We'll just have to push on harder. Keep your eyes open, and your guns handy. We may need them sooner than you think. Ol' Ezra'd be the kind to think of an ambush, and the boy might just be headin' smack into the middle of it," Tauber said, as he spurred his horse to a trot. The six others fell in line as the sheriff led them across the knoll where Johnny had first spotted them coming.

As Johnny followed the trail of the stolen horse, the shadows of a waning day crept up the canyon walls, making tracking more and more difficult. He knew he would have to stop and make camp soon. The light snow cover gave the canyon an eerie, peaceful quiet. Nervous tension sent electricity through Johnny's body as he became acutely aware of each ringing clack of the gray's hooves, and his imagination exaggerated the sound as it seemed to echo off the steep granite walls like metallic thunder.

His accentuated awareness of every step his horse took, made him as equally alert to the fact that his adversary, too, would not be deaf to approaching sounds. He wished he had a way to wrap his horse's feet, Indian-style, to give him the advantage of silence and, thus, surprise. Surprise could mean the difference between life and death. Life obviously meant little to the man who rode ahead of him. Hadn't he taken Simon's life for a few dollars and a horse?

Johnny tried to imagine who could be up there, only a few hours ahead of him. Was it someone he knew? Or perhaps merely a drifter, a saddle tramp who figured to slip into town, unnoticed, steal enough to take him a few days further down his road to nowhere, then slip away like a phantom in the night? Maybe Simon surprised the intruder and was killed in the ensuing panic of having been caught. No, panic doesn't sneak up and stab you in the back. Besides, how would a drifter know that Simon didn't trust banks? It could only be someone from town who knew about Simon's cash box, and my knife, he thought, and that means I know him. The thought sent a chill through him.

The snow fell with increasing intensity the higher into the mountains he rode. The winds picked up and swirled the white powder like eddies in a stream, lifting and moving, constantly rearranging the landscape. The trail Johnny followed, too, was slowly being obliterated until he could no longer be sure he was even following a trail. He thought of giving up the chase several times, but he heard the voice inside telling him, *Keep going; you don't need a trail; you'll know how to find him.*

The voice was not new to him. He'd heard it many times before, and it provided valuable advice without fail. His mother had said it was the voice of an ancestor protecting him from evil. He never believed that as anything more than some old Indian tale.

But this time was different. This time it was more powerful than anything he'd ever felt. This time, his very life could be held in the balance. He straightened in the saddle and rode on, following the voice in his head, and a vanishing trail.

A cold, steady breeze now began to slide down into the canyon and Johnny knew it was going to be a bitterly cold night. He dared not build a fire for fear of detection. As far as he knew, the killer did not know of his presence, but a fire would surely eliminate any possible element of surprise. The trail, now vague, seemed to lead upwards along an incline toward a wide ledge, so he decided to seek refuge for a time beneath a clump of junipers at the base of the slope, near an outcropping of boulders.

He staked the gray out just below the rocks, then began scraping away loose dirt and gravel from beneath an immense granite ledge that jutted nearly horizontally from the slope. It would suffice as a temporary shelter from the weather. A heavy wool blanket would afford protection from the biting wind that was beginning to increase in intensity as a dark, ominous, swirling cloud cover swallowed up the peaks, slipping steadily down the sides of the canyon walls like thick maple syrup over a stack of hotcakes.

Looking up toward the ledge, he could barely make out a dark hole where a long abandoned lode mine probably had been located. A slag pile spewed from its mouth and tumbled down the mountainside like lava. An old mine would be a good place for someone to hide in ambush of anyone foolish enough to get too nosy, and Johnny decided to scout out that possibility well after the gray sky had turned to the pitch black of night. Without a moon, the going would be tough and he would have to hike on foot as one misstep on horseback could mean a drop of several hundred feet down jagged rocks to the inhospitable floor below. First, however, he needed sleep, and, finding a flat piece of shale, finished smoothing the soft, sandy loam.

He covered the bare dirt with pine needles and fallen aspen leaves and settled back with his blanket wrapped around him to await a time when he would least be expected to ascend the trail. As he huddled in his shallow cave, he listened, and waited for the silence that would reassure him that his position was more secure than he felt right then. Being between a posse and a killer, either of whom could come upon him at any time, kept him nervously alert and he knew sleep wouldn't come easily.

Trees and shrubs, crackling objection to the whistling wind and blowing snow, and the mournful screech of a mountain lion filled the canyon with its only night sounds. The biting chill carried his thoughts up the trail to that black hole in the canyon wall. He felt certain that Simon's killer was, by now, sitting in front of a crackling fire, set well back in the mine shaft to avoid giving away his position, warm and comfortable — too comfortable, Johnny hoped — and thus would be off guard. He pulled the Colt from his belt and held it in his hand to calm his fears. The power he carried in that six-shooter gave him comfort and he drifted off to sleep.

"It's getting dark . . . and colder, Sheriff," one of the townsfolk-turned-posse complained after many hours in the saddle.

"I got a family that needs me, and chores to 'tend to," said another. "We should just turn back, we'll never find him in those treacherous passes anyway, especially in the dead of night. We ain't prepared proper for a long trek."

Sheriff Tauber halted the line of grumbling men, turned in his saddle, and pushed his hat back on his head with an impatient sigh.

Things were certain to get harder. He'd be better off to go it alone than be saddled with a bunch of whiners.

"If any of you want to go back, you know the way. I guess it really isn't your job to find Ezra, it's mine. So, go on back. Macmillan, you watch things for me 'til I return, and consider yourself still deputized," he said, singling out the only one of the bunch he knew he could count on: The head of the volunteer fire department.

The group all looked at each other, nodded, hastily turned their horses about and set off, single file, back toward town. None hesitated to accept the sheriff's offer. They wouldn't be missed.

Sheriff Tauber sat momentarily gazing ahead to the great granite peaks in the distance. His thoughts of what might lie ahead consumed him. *Looks like it's just you and me now, Johnny. I hope I'll not be too late to keep you from bein' another victim to this desperate man.*

Damn, it's gettin' cold and I'm goin' to have to make camp, soon. Reckon I'll try to make it to the mouth of Black Canyon Pass, and bed down there for the night. He pulled the collar of his heavy sheepskin coat up high around his neck and buttoned the first four buttons to protect against the sharp wind that licked at his face. Flexing his right hand to relieve the dull pain brought on by the cold, he tugged the brim of his hat down low on his forehead and urged his horse on, wishing it was a month earlier when the nights were still warm and clear.

CHAPTER THIRTEEN

Johnny stirred from his blankets an hour before dawn, before the sky began its gradual change from cold black to warm gray. He knew the time was at hand for him to make his way to the mouth of the old mine, there to identify, and confront, if necessary, whoever had killed his friend, Simon. He saddled the gray, then rolled his blankets together and tied them with the rawhide strings to the skirt of the saddle. Though he would be climbing the mountain on foot, he wanted the horse ready if he had to get out of there in a hurry. One wrap of the reins around a low aspen limb would be sufficient to guarantee the horse still being there when he returned.

He pulled a pair of gloves from a saddlebag and put them on, then drew the Colt from his belt to assure himself that it was still loaded. Regarding his keen affinity for the revolver, he wondered if he could actually use it to shoot another man. Taking a deep breath, he started his long climb toward the mine.

Johnny saw that the tracks leading up to the mine entrance were still discernible in the light snow, and he realized that if they were that clear to him, any tracks he made would be even clearer to anyone looking down, so he decided to take to the rocks that jutted from the rugged sides of the pass and approach the opening from above. The route would be dangerous, as one mistake could send a small avalanche of rocks and debris down onto the canyon floor, noisily announcing his arrival to whomever awaited him, unless, of course, he lost his footing as well, becoming part of the avalanche and tumbling the several hundred feet to the rock base of the canyon, whereupon he would be of little concern to anyone.

He began the climb, making his way slowly, taking care to avoid moving too hastily lest his impatience prove his undoing. It was difficult for a young man to be patient and he had to practice, with every step he took, the forbearance his mother had taught him as a youth in Kansas. He took comfort from her words, and from the .45 Colt stuffed in his belt.

As the sky grew lighter, the night breeze

turned to gusty winds that swirled stinging sand and bitterly cold snow against his face. He knew when the sun broke through the overcast, he'd warm up quickly in the thin air of the high altitude. But, the lighter it got, the easier he'd be to spot sneaking up to the abandoned mine. He couldn't be both warm and well hidden. He made do by pulling his red kerchief up around his nose and mouth to avoid eating any more sand and dirt than necessary, and to keep some of the chill out of his lungs.

Having stopped only twice to catch his breath, he finally reached a point just above the mine entrance from which he felt he could make his way down to the very edge of the exposed timbers at the opening. From there, he wasn't sure what he was going to do. He only knew it was too late to turn back for he was too close to his quarry. From his new vantage point, he clearly saw the tracks he'd been following lead directly to the mine.

Slowly, each step studied and tested to ensure he would not slip in the gravel and loose dirt that covered the ground above the opening, he edged ever closer to the entrance. He was about five feet above the beams that erupted from, and, he hoped, supported, the ground on which he was standing. Just as he went into a crouching position to ease down to the mine entrance, he heard the distinctive sound of dry-rotted wood cracking under his weight. The wood had thoroughly decayed from years of exposure to freezing and thawing, and the timber suddenly collapsed under him, sending him head over heels to the hard-packed dirt and rocks several feet below. He came crashing down with such force as to completely knock the wind out of him. He lay momentarily unconscious.

The sound of Johnny's plunge to the ground amidst gravel and slag, not to mention the cracking timber, brought Ezra Goode to his feet in a flash. Certain he'd been discovered, he grabbed his sidearm from its holster near his bedroll and fired blindly toward the entrance of the shaft. Two quick shots echoed deep into the mountainside, then all fell silent. Hearing no return gunfire, he carefully made his way toward the gray light emanating from the opening about twenty feet away.

Gun drawn and ready, he poked his head out into the gray light of dawn, only to see Johnny Beaver flat on his back, unmoving, his left arm bent unnaturally beneath him.

"Well how 'bout this, a damned redskin just dropped in fer an uninvited visit. Sorry, but I'm just not in an entertainin' mood," he said as he pointed the .44 at Johnny's head and cocked the hammer full back.

Ezra's earlier shots had caught the attention of Sheriff Tauber, who had gotten an early start following the tracks into the canyon, and was about halfway up the incline when the commotion began. He was in a position to see Ezra emerge from the mine entrance, gun in hand. Though he hadn't known what the old man had been shooting at, Tauber had seen the horse Johnny had likely been riding at the bottom of the grade. Figuring Johnny might have been the target, Tauber hastily raised his Winchester carbine and fired. His ricocheting shot missed Ezra, but drew the old man's attention away from the fallen boy. Ezra spun around and wildly returned fire as he ducked behind a large boulder at the top of the path.

Johnny came to his senses in time to see someone crouching behind the rocks, lying in wait for someone or something. Johnny couldn't make out who the shadowy figure was, but he knew instinctively he was about to witness an ambush. As his vision began to clear, he realized, as he attempted to move, that his left arm was probably broken. He fell back, exhausted. After all he'd been through, he was ready to give up and just lie there. He hurt too much to care anymore.

But, the voice inside his head wouldn't leave him alone. *Someone needs your help, get up! Now!* Startled by the clarity of those words coming from nowhere, he tried as hard as he could to shake off the fog in his head. The voice came again. *You can do it. You must!* It sounded like Simon. He would try.

Summoning all his strength, Johnny found he was able to raise up sufficiently to make out the identity of the figure with the gun. *Ezra Goode! That's who must have killed Simon!* A flood of repeated warnings over several years from Simon that Ezra was a worthless and dangerous man, a killer — a man to steer clear of — came rushing back.

Then, out of the corner of his eye, he saw his friend, the sheriff, about to be Ezra's next victim. He couldn't let that happen. With his right hand, he very carefully and very slowly, eased the Colt from his belt and placed his thumb on the hammer. He knew the click would alert Ezra to his action, so he waited for some noise, any noise, that might cover the sound of his cocking the gun. It came in short order. In the form of another shot from Tauber's rifle aimed at keeping Ezra pinned down, ricocheting from the rock just above Ezra's position.

Tauber was in a precarious position himself, as he was halfway up the trail with no cover, only a sheer drop-off to one side and a vertical wall of granite on the other.

Ezra eased back just inside the upright timber at the entrance, to give himself a perfect shot at the man below. He finally had the sheriff nearly in his sights. He drew careful aim.

Johnny had to act quickly. "Ezra!" he shouted. He fired as the old man spun around in response. The blast from the Colt slammed Ezra to the ground with such force that the .44 was thrown from his hand. Johnny's bullet had struck the surprised man in the center of his chest, and he lay gasping for air. Blood spurted from the wound, spreading over his woolen undershirt like fresh bread soaking up thin gravy. Droplets of crimson pooled on the ground beside him. Johnny struggled to get to his feet, but he couldn't bring himself to approach the dying man.

Just as Tauber made it to where the pathetic old man lay, Ezra coughed and died. The grizzled con man left this world wearing only a pair of worn-out socks, dirty denim pants and woolen longhandles, now dyed red from the massive chest wound he'd suffered.

The sheriff stood, regarding the body with disgust for the miserable life the old reprobate had led. He then turned to find Johnny gazing emptily down into the canyon, the Colt lay in the dirt where it flew from his hand after firing the fatal shot. Tauber picked it up, then walked over and handed it back to the boy.

"Thanks, Johnny, you just saved my skin," Tauber said. He then noticed the boy's twisted arm dangling uselessly. "We'll have to make a sling for that arm, and get you back to where it can be set proper. Stay here and I'll get the horses and bring 'em up. I'll round up the one Ezra stole from the livery, to haul his sorry carcass back to town."

When the sheriff returned, he was able to fashion a sling from the rawhide ropes securing Johnny's bedroll, then hoist him into the saddle of the gray. Johnny hadn't said a word as they started backtracking the trail toward town. He seemed in a daze. The bay mare brought up the rear with Ezra's limp body draped over the saddle, covered with a blanket. Tauber had secured the money stolen from Simon and, as far as he was concerned, the incident was over. But, in Johnny's mind, it all hadn't quite come together.

"I didn't do it. I could never hurt Simon. He was sorta like a —"

"Father?" Sheriff Tauber finished. "Of course you didn't do it, no one ever thought you did."

"But, my knife killed him and —"

"You thought we'd assume it was you, right?"

"Reckon so." Johnny hung his head.

"Ezra cheated a banker from St. Louis out of a lot of money. He'd been doing it for quite a spell. The banker filed a complaint, and before I could arrest Ezra, he'd gone to see the banker and killed him. Ezra'd lost his last cent gambling, and since he knew I'd be hot after him for killin' the banker, he needed money, quick. Like nearly everyone in town, he knew Simon kept cash at the livery, so he robbed and killed Simon too." Tauber turned in his saddle to look back at Johnny. "Nobody thought you'd done a thing wrong. Fact is, we figured you'd picked up Ezra's trail and was headed out after him yourself."

"You did?"

"Yep. And since you're the one that killed him, reckon you'll be a hero back in town."

Johnny sat up straighter in his saddle at the comment, then he looked down at the

Colt the sheriff had stuck back in his belt and wondered if he really could have gone into that cave, confronted Ezra for Simon's death, and tried to bring him in alive. The way he was feeling at that moment, he didn't think so. He didn't feel much like a hero. Killing the old man, even with good reason, was creating an awful feeling in the pit of his stomach. He thought he might even get sick.

"You know, Johnny, someone's gonna have to run that livery, an' I think Simon would've wanted it to be you. I'd say your future's secure in Lake City." The sheriff smiled, then spurred the black horse on to pick up the pace. He hoped to be back in town by late evening and the thought of even day-old coffee was mighty appealing in the chilly morning air.

Several weeks passed before Johnny's arm healed and he could again take notice of the nickel-plated Colt Peacemaker. He pulled it from a drawer where he'd placed it the very day he returned. He sat gazing at the beautifully crafted weapon. He held it for a minute, then half-cocked the hammer, and rolled the cylinder through several times. Four bullets remained, unused. He rewrapped the gun in a red kerchief, then placed it back in the drawer.

Two weeks later, Johnny walked into John Tauber's office and laid the gun, still wrapped in the kerchief, on the desk. "Sheriff, I'm leaving this with you. I don't think I'll be needin' it." Tauber unwrapped the Colt. He understood that Johnny now saw the Colt as an object that brought death, not freedom. He looked up and said, "I wish more men felt the way you do."

Johnny nodded and turned to leave, he felt good about his decision to get rid of the .45. "Sell it if you've a mind to, Sheriff," Johnny said over his shoulder as he left the sheriff's office. The voice had told him what to do. He was whistling as he started across the street.

Sheriff Tauber did sell the Colt soon thereafter. A collector of unusual handguns happened to hear of the gun with the ivory rattlesnake on the grips, and made a special effort to seek out its whereabouts. John Edward Pomeroy, a businessman from Omaha on his way back home from San Francisco, offered $100 for it. Sold. Tauber was happy to rid himself of an object that elicited memories of the likes of Creeg Bedloe and Ezra Goode.

CHAPTER FOURTEEN

November, 1877

The Omaha-Lincoln stagecoach stood at the edge of a muddy, rutted road twenty miles outside of Lincoln, Nebraska, late one cold afternoon. The driver, guard and two passengers stood beside the coach with their hands in the air. The guard's rifle lay on the ground in front of him. Two men walked back and forth in front of the four nervous detainees. One was slim, well-dressed, sporting a trailduster and brandishing a sawed-off, double-barreled shotgun. The other was a flabby, child-like giant wearing a sheepskin coat with sleeves that were too short.

"Shoot the lock off that strongbox, baby brother," the man in the trailduster said, "then, put the cash in these." He threw two sets of leather saddlebags on the ground in front of the big one.

"Yessir, Gar, I'll do just that." Hastily, he

did as he was told. After he had filled the bags, he froze in place as if he couldn't decide what to do next. He looked to his partner for further instructions. None came. The man in the long coat had been distracted by the sight of a fancy mahogany box with brass corner trim sitting on the floor inside the coach.

"What's in the box?" he asked the passengers.

A man wearing a business suit under a stylish fox coat answered, "Just, ah, some things I collect. Nothing of any value, I assure you."

"Open it!" the bandit ordered.

"Please, sir, there's nothing of importance to anyone but myself."

The holdup man's patience came to an abrupt end as he suddenly brought the stock of the shotgun around and up, striking the surprised passenger in the face with a brutal blow. The man dropped instantly to the ground with a grunt, blood spurting from his grotesquely broken nose.

"Want I should fetch the box, Gar?" Rufe asked eagerly.

"Yeah. This gent ain't been too helpful."

The big one dragged the heavy case through the open door of the coach and let it crash to the ground. It split open as the impact destroyed the fragile lock, dumping its contents onto the snow.

"Guns, Gar! It's full of guns!" he shouted as he instinctively reached down for the first revolver that tumbled from the box. He snatched up a nickel-plated Colt with childish glee. Then the other bandit tore it from his hand, attracted by the unusual carved ivory inlay in the grips.

He turned it over, cocked it, felt its fine balance, ran his fingers over the unusual snake on the ivory grips. Gar was at once entranced by this fine weapon. This would be his weapon of choice from now on, he thought.

"Please, sir, I beg of you —" the owner of the case protested, stumbling in an attempt to get back on his feet as he pulled a small caliber pistol from his coat pocket. He was unable to defend himself or plead his case further. The roar of the Colt caught John Edward Pomeroy in the face, ending any further need he might have had for the shiny Colt Peacemaker with the rattlesnake inlay.

June, 1878

The frontier town of North Platte, Nebraska was unusually calm for a Thursday afternoon, with few homesteaders seeing the need to venture into town midweek. Most everyone was tending to their fields. This was the first year since '74 that the swarms of grasshoppers had not invaded, devouring the crops and forcing many settlers to head back east, discouraged and reduced to poverty.

An intense sun blazed down on the wide dirt streets, convincing most of the townsfolk to seek shelter indoors, finding chores that could be done under more comfortable conditions. With the heat came a strange, disquieting stillness, like a calm before some unseen storm. But no storm appeared on the horizon, and only the constant wind or an occasional wagon, rattling down the dusty street, broke the silence of the plains.

On the porch of the single-story sheriff's office and jail, stood Sheriff Thomas Morgan talking to his son, US Marshal JT "Ivory John" Morgan. Ivory John was visiting his father for a few days on his way from Omaha to a new appointment in the Arizona territory.

"Not a bad town you've got here, Dad. Too bad I can't stay around a while longer," Ivory John said. He sat casually in a creaky, spindle-back chair leaning against the whipsaw siding of the building with his feet up on the porch railing. His long legs were clad in black pants that he tucked inside high-top, black boots. "I could sure use some peace and quiet for a spell."

"It's not always this peaceful," the old sheriff responded. Making a move toward the steps, he lifted his straw hat and wiped perspiration from his forehead with his sleeve, then mopped the sweatband with a red handkerchief retrieved from a back pocket. Replacing the kerchief, he tugged at a silver watch fob dangling from the pocket of his well-worn wool vest, fishing out a gold-plated timepiece. He opened the watch's cover and then snapped it closed, replacing it in the same frayed pocket in which it had resided for nearly ten years.

"Noon. Time to stroll over to the bank and make sure the money shipment from Lincoln gets there okay. How about goin' along, son? I'd kinda like you to meet Missy Andrews, the bank manager's daughter. Right sweet little gal. Been tellin' her about you for two years, now, and she seems mighty interested. Wouldn't hurt none for you to consider settlin' down, you know."

Ivory John blushed and looked down briefly at the badge that hung from his blue shirt. "I appreciate what you're tryin' to do, but I don't reckon any woman'd put up for long with the sorta life I lead. Bein' a lawman's not an easy way for a woman, never knowin' where her man is, or even if he's alive. Not sure I'm ready to put anyone through that. You understand, don't you, Dad?"

"Reckon I do. Your ma never really favored this life, neither. Maybe that's part of what took her away from us so early." Tom placed his hand on his son's shoulder. "Do as you please; I'll be back in 'bout an hour and we'll fetch us some grub." The sheriff stepped into the street, heading for the bank two blocks away.

Ivory John nodded, pulled his dark blue, cavalry-style Stetson down low on his forehead, then folded his arms across his chest. The young marshal stroked his bushy blond mustache and watched the old man walk away, remembering the many times as a youth he'd seen his father step off similar porches to go settle some dispute or stop a drunk from destroying a saloon. Sheriff Tom had gotten into close quarters on more than one occasion during his long tenure as a peace officer, and Ivory John counted himself lucky his father had survived those post-war years when hell was a synonym for many a frontier town. The rush to settle the territory had brought with it much more than good farm folks looking for a piece of land. Along with the crowds of eager settlers came the lowlifes, scoundrels, thieves and killers, looking for easy pickings and a disorganized, powerless law. He was happy the old sheriff was finally settled in a town as civilized as North Platte.

CHAPTER FIFTEEN

"Now you best remember what I told you, Rufe," Gar Baker said to his younger brother. "That goes for you, too, Hicks. Now mind you don't go and cross me, neither of you."

"I ain't never crossed you, Gar. You know that," Rufe cried with a hurt look on his fat, sunburned face.

"Me neither," Hicks jumped in sarcastically.

Gar swung around in his saddle, his eyes ablaze with sudden anger. "Then what'd you go and kill that sodbuster back in Gothenburg for after I told you not to? You better start doin' what I say or so help me, Hicks, I'll blow you away myself. You understand?" He pulled the gleaming Colt .45 from his holster and aimed it straight at Hicks. Hicks held up both hands in mock surrender.

"Yessir, *Mr.* Gar Baker. Whatever you say.

But I say that damn sodbuster needed killin' for gettin' so all het up over me just wantin' a little kiss from that purty red-haired gal of his."

Dalton Hicks crossed his hands on the pommel of his saddle and grinned at Gar with nearly black teeth. He carried a wad of chewing tobacco in his cheek constantly, even while eating. He turned his head and spat, then wiped his mouth across a brown-stained sleeve. His drab pants and red suspenders gave him the look of any other settler in the area, concealing his true nature, that of a cold-blooded killer with a propensity for sudden, irrational outbursts that often ended in murder. Only his gun-belt full of cartridges and a converted .44 Remington gave hint of that side of him.

He had first become a wanted man eight years earlier in Missouri for slitting the throat of his uncle for $200 in gold coins he found in the uncle's desk. Since that time, no one knew just how many others had been added to his list, but by the time someone realized who he was, it was often already too late for them.

The Baker brothers were worse in their own way. The cynical older brother, Gar, plotted and schemed his way all over Missouri, Iowa and Nebraska, robbing banks, trains and stagecoaches, generally hitting whichever he figured would have the most cash at the time. He'd killed his share of men, too, but he preferred just to grab the money and run. And running was something he'd grown quite adept at; the cunning Gar Baker wouldn't easily give up his freedom. A thready man with narrow shoulders, he sat straight in the saddle, a slit-eyed stare ever on his gaunt face. A sparse mustache sat above thin lips that never smiled. Wearing a tan trailduster to protect his clothes from the ravages of the prairie dust, he took great pride in being well dressed, often buying whole new outfits with his ill-gotten loot. A fancy new suit seemed to boost his ego to even greater heights than usual; he liked the smell of new clothes, a fresh shave and plenty of rose water. The only thing he never changed was his black felt derby hat, won from a drummer in Lincoln during a poker game. A white-tipped hawk feather adorned the silk band. Though he certainly dressed the part of a "dandy," he gunned down one man just for calling him one.

It was nearing noon. As the three men neared North Platte, Gar rehearsed the other two in the parts they were to play in the next few hours. Their destinies depended on strict adherence to the long thought-out plans of their self-appointed leader. "One more time, what do you do when we approach the bank, Rufe?"

"Uh, I get off my horse and go sit on the bench outside the door to the bank. If the sheriff comes, I run in and tell you." The big man got a puzzled look on his face, then said, "Gar, what do I do if they's already a body on the bench?"

"You stupid ox —" Hicks blurted out in frustration.

"Shut up, Hicks! Now, Rufe, if the bench is bein' used, you can jus stand by the door and watch. And don't fergit, when we come out, you got to fetch all three horses because we'll be carryin' a lotta heavy bags. Can you remember all that?" Gar spoke patiently to his younger brother.

Rufe had been born several weeks prematurely, the result of a wagon accident that caused his mother to go into early labor. She died in childbirth, and, for the many people whose lives had been adversely affected by Rufe's actions since, it would have been just as well if he had died along with her. He had the mind of a four-year-old, and the body of a bear — three hundred pounds, six-feet-two, with arms like railroad ties. His moods changed with sudden, violent tantrums that erupted without warning. He once strangled a dog for barking at him as he tried to pet it. He had killed three men with his bare hands after getting roaring drunk one Saturday night in Dubuque, Iowa and was sentenced to hang for the crime. Brother Gar broke him out of jail a day before the hanging and the two of them made a quick exit out of the state, heading for Nebraska and hoped-for anonymity.

"Uh huh. I can 'member, Gar. Whatever's told me, I can 'member." Rufe grinned big and raised both eyebrows to Hicks.

Hicks' eyes narrowed at the sight of the giant; his hatred of Rufe brought a knot to his stomach. He dreamed of ways to rid himself of this buffoon, this babbling idiot he figured would someday get him killed. But for the time being, he would remain silent as best he could. For now, he needed Gar, the planner. He figured soon he'd have the wherewithal to break away on his own, head for Mexico and live the good life off the spoils of the only career he'd really ever known: Taking from others what was rightfully theirs.

"Awright, Hicks, whadda *you* do?"

"While you keep everone covered, I get the bank manager to open the safe and load the cash into bags. I toss the money to you to start carryin' out and I grab the manager's daughter for a hostage. You and Rufe lead out with the money and I follow with the gal up behind me, so they won't be shootin' at us for fear of hittin' her." Hicks turned to Rufe and gave him a self-righteous nod. "We head south across the grasslands toward Medicine Creek. That backwards prairie town'll never know what hit them. Anythin' else you need to know?" he sneered.

"That about covers it. Oh, remember, Hicks, no harm comes to the gal. Got that? We'll let her go about ten miles south of town. We don't need nobody slowin' us down. By then, they're gonna have a home-town posse out after us, and when they find her safe, more than likely half of them'll turn back."

The sun was nearly straight up as the three entered the city limits and rode slowly down the main street. As they reined-in in front of the North Platte Settler's Bank, they eased off their saddles. Gar and Hicks each handed their reins to Rufe then entered the double doors at the front of the modest, single-story, stone building. Once inside, Gar drew the Colt and shouted, "Everbody get yer hands in the air or I'll blow yer heads off."

Hicks slammed through the fragile swinging door that led behind the tellers' cages, drew his revolver, and pointed it at the forehead of the startled bank manager. His daughter, Missy, screamed and Hicks slapped her across the face, hard. She fell back against the desk, then slipped to the floor, dazed.

"Get that damn vault open, mister, and start fillin' them bags, quick, or the little gal here gets a bullet," Hicks growled. The bewildered manager stumbled over his own chair in his haste to reach the vault, holding up one hand while reaching for the lock dial with the other.

"Don't hurt her, please. I-I'll get you the money, just don't hurt Missy," the manager begged, fumbling with the combination. Once the vault was open, Hicks pushed the man aside. When he could see inside the vault, he stepped back in shock. There were only three stacks of bills and five bags of coins on the shelf.

"Gar! Dammit, Gar, there ain't no money here like you promised! No more'n a few hundred in bills!" Hicks shouted across the room to a surprised Gar Baker, whose perfect plan appeared to be going awry. Hicks turned to the manager, sprawled on the floor, trying to scoot away from the angry gunman. "Where the hell's the money, old man? Supposed to be ten thousand here!"

"It-it's due any minute on the stage from Lincoln. It's noon, shoulda been here a half-hour ago," the manager stammered.

"Whatta we do, now, Gar?"

"Shut up! Lemme think." The blank look on Gar's face told everyone in the bank the same story: He didn't know what to do next. That made him even more dangerous. He wiped the perspiration from his face with his hand, his eyes darted about as if searching for an answer written on the walls or on the faces of the three customers who stood, hands raised, against the wall.

"We can't wait, the sheriff might come. Grab what you can, let's get outta here, NOW! And leave them damn coins, they're too heavy!" Gar yelled across the room to Hicks, then reached up and snatched a small leather wallet from one of the customers who held it in his raised hands. "What's in here, sodbuster?"

"T-twenty dollars, sir," the quivering man said. Gar stuffed it in his belt, then moving to the next man, reached inside the man's coat and yanked a wallet from an inside pocket. He tore the paper bills from inside, stuffed the few measly dollars in his pocket, and threw the empty wallet to the floor. He passed up the third customer, a short, fat woman with squinty eyes and a scowl that suggested she'd be more trouble than whatever money she had was worth grabbing.

Hicks gathered all the money he could find in the tellers' drawers into the three bags, tossed them over the cage to Gar, then seized Missy by the arm and yanked her off the floor. All one hundred pounds of her. "Yer comin' with us, sweety. If you cause us any grief, yer pappy'll never see you alive again."

Just as the pair started backing toward the door, Sheriff Morgan entered the bank, totally unaware of what had transpired. Failure to grasp the situation quickly proved his undoing, for as the sheriff stopped, motionless, for the briefest moment, Gar spun around and instinctively fired the nickel-plated Colt. The shot caught the sheriff straight-on in the middle of his chest, catapulting him backward through the etched Victorian window. Glass crashed about him as his body crumpled to the wooden sidewalk at Rufe's feet. Rufe lumbered to the door just as Gar and Hicks came bursting out, nearly knocking him down in their hasty retreat.

"You was s'posed to tell us if the sheriff come, you stupid jackass!" Hicks yelled at

Rufe, as all three of them scrambled to untie the horses and get mounted. Hicks almost pulled Missy's arm out of the socket as he hauled her up behind him.

Gar was the first to spur his horse, and, clinging tightly to one of the three sacks of money, he managed to head the horse at full gallop down the street and toward the grasslands to the south. Rufe's horse followed closely behind, as the big man clutched the other two bags closely to his chest with one beefy arm. Hicks brought up the rear, as planned, with the frightened girl kicking and pounding on his back, screaming for him to let her go.

Chapter Sixteen

Ivory John Morgan had been inside the sheriff's office when he heard the shot from two blocks down. He jumped up from the desk, scattering wanted dodgers onto the floor, and ran outside. When he saw people running toward the bank, he joined them, reaching the front of the building as a crowd was forming. He pushed through the wall of gasping onlookers, then stopped, horrified at the sight that lay before him. His father was lying on his back, covered with broken glass and blood. Ivory John knelt beside the gasping man, reached under his shoulders and gently lifted, cradling him in his arms. The sheriff couldn't speak. The wounds were fatal and they both knew it. Tom's eyes showed no pain, just a searching for the why of it all, then, they glazed over as he gave one last gasp and died in his son's arms. Ivory John gazed down at the face of the man whose whole life had been devoted to the law. Now, someone had ripped that life away in the blink of an eye. Sorrow and anger began to well up, intermingling inside the young marshal's brain, swirling around, making it difficult to distinguish one from the other. Finally, anger won out. Several of the men came forward out of the crowd to lift the old sheriff off the wooden sidewalk and carry him to the undertaker's parlor. Ivory John stood staring after them for a moment, then, pushing his way into the bank, came face to face with the distraught bank manager who was leaning shakily on his desk, and whimpering.

"Missy. You've got to find Missy. They took her. She's all I have. Please," he pleaded with the first person he saw wearing a badge: Ivory John Morgan.

Several of the men who had gathered at the scene of the shooting spoke up.

"We'll go with you, Marshal."

"If you need to get a posse together, you can count on me."

"We'll get our horses and be ready in ten minutes." They all seemed to Ivory John to be speaking at once. He held up his hand to quiet the crowd.

A man stepped forward and said, "I've seen them three on wanted posters in the sheriff's office. It'd be the Baker brothers and Dalton Hicks. I'm sure of it."

Ivory John stiffened at the news. He knew of all three of them, and he knew he'd be in for a tough ride. He'd wanted to see them captured and strung up for a long time.

"Be obliged if those of you that can afford to be away for a time'd get your horses, guns, and provisions for two or three days, then meet me in front of the jail," he said, struggling to be the man-in-charge they all expected him to be.

He was numb from the sudden loss of his father. He quickly removed himself from the slowly dispersing crowd and made for the jail, searching for answers as he went. *This isn't going to be easy,* he thought, *not with the anger that is trying to get hold of me. How can I be a lawman under these circumstances? If the posse should demand we string up those three, how do I separate the fire in my gut from the job? I'm not sure I'm up to bein' a lawman right now. Not sure at all.*

Ivory John had his black gelding saddled and ready in front of the jail as five other men approached, ready for the pursuit. "Men, I'm swearing you in as deputies. As such, you are as bound to abide by the law as if you wore the badge. Is that clear to all of you? If it isn't, better clear out now. I'll not have any lynch-mob sorts with me." He said the words although they felt empty. He hoped no one noticed. He looked each of them straight in the eye, and, not seeing anyone turn away, swung into his saddle and spurred the black horse to action. Six men rode hard into the grasslands, following a fresh trail, not knowing what lay ahead, but hoping they'd be ready when the time came.

Almost two hours had passed since the robbery, and the three desperate men had relentlessly pushed their mounts nearly the whole time. Gar figured they'd put enough distance between themselves and any posse, so he reined-in his well-lathered horse under a stand of trees by a small creek. "Water yer animals, and rest a spell. Another few miles we'll be at Medicine Creek. Camp there for the night," he said, slipping from the heaving animal's back.

"Where we headed, Gar?" Hicks asked as he dropped from his saddle, pulling the still whimpering girl down with him. "We still goin' to Colorado?"

"Don't you worry none about that, Hicks. Just you cover our backsides."

Rufe waited until Gar specifically told him to dismount, then he thundered to the ground like a giant child jumping off a porch, twisting his ankle in the process.

"Owww!" Rufe howled.

"Whut happened?" Gar asked.

"Hurt m' foot, Gar."

"When you gonna learn to get off a horse, you stupid oaf?" Hicks mocked. He picked up a small stone and flung it in Rufe's direction. Rufe ducked awkwardly, nearly falling in the stream.

"Tell him to quit callin' me names, Gar," Rufe whined.

"Leave him be, Hicks. He can't help it." Gar shook his head in disbelief at the crew with which he had saddled himself.

"Whut about this purty little gal?" Hicks said, leering at Missy. She turned from him, nervously crossing her arms in front of her as she took several steps backward.

"She stays. Don't need her no more," Gar said. "From now on, we don't need nuthin' slowin' us down. Now water yer mount and let's get goin'."

Leaving his horse beside the stream, Hicks went to where Missy Andrews sat, shaking, huddled in the tall grass. She was staring forlornly back toward North Platte. Tears had made trails in the dust on her delicate face. He squatted beside her, reaching out to run his grimy hand down her long, silky black hair. Usually swirled on top in a bun and secured with a silver comb, her hair had fallen loose during the struggle and now cascaded in a tangle down the center of her back.

"Don't touch me, you filthy animal," she said as she slapped at his hand, recoiling from the unpleasant sensation. Her inability to hide her revulsion made her even more vulnerable. Her green eyes erupted with tears just looking at him. His touch made her skin crawl. Hicks just grinned broadly, showing those near-black teeth. He'd been rejected by women all his life; Missy Andrews was no different than all the others.

"Leave her alone, Hicks! Git mounted and move out," Gar said angrily. He never liked the tobacco-chewing degenerate, and Gar was at the limit of his patience with him. He had kept Hicks around mainly because of the man's considerable skill with a gun. Beyond that, he'd considered shooting him before he became more of a liability.

The three mounted up and started in-trail to the south toward Medicine Creek and a more secure place to camp for the night. Gar had used it as a hiding place before. Missy was left to fend for herself in the middle of the prairie.

After riding about ten minutes, Hicks said, "Damn, I musta dropped my watch by the creek. Go on ahead, I'll just ride back and fetch it. I'll catch up in a few minutes."

"Don't you be gettin' no ideas about that gal. Jus get yer watch and hightail it back, you understand?" Gar bellowed.

Hicks wheeled his horse about and threw Gar a wave as he backtracked at a gallop toward the stream they'd just left.

Missy was struggling to make her way back toward town; hiking up her long skirt and trying to avoid twisting an ankle on the uneven, rocky ground. Her high-heeled, high-button shoes made the going difficult. She was terrified by the thought of spending the night in the wilderness alone, with no protection, not even a blanket. She heard the pounding of hooves behind her, and, as she turned, hoping to see a rescuer, she realized that her plight had gone from bad to worse. Her heart pounded in desperation. It was Hicks! He'd come back and she didn't even have the bellowing Gar Baker to keep some semblance of control over this degenerate. Terrified, she tried to run, wildly waving her arms and shouting, hoping that somehow, someone might hear her cry for help. The wind, the screech of a circling hawk, and the pounding of the horse's hooves were the only other sounds to accompany her panicked flight. She stumbled and fell to the ground, gasping for air after only a few futile minutes of trying to escape her determined pursuer.

Hicks jumped from his horse before even coming to a complete halt, grabbing the sobbing girl as she struggled to escape his disgusting grip. She screamed and clawed at his face in desperation as he began slapping her repeatedly. Missy closed her eyes and prayed for a miracle to save her. She was quickly knocked unconscious by his savage attack.

Looking down on her frail form sprawled in the grass, Hicks hissed, "No damned woman's gonna get away with looking at me like I was dirt."

Assuming he'd killed her with the beating, Hicks calmly rode off after his partners in crime.

CHAPTER SEVENTEEN

Ivory John and the makeshift posse were making good time through the tall prairie grass, following an easy trail as long as they kept no more than the hour or so behind they had steadily maintained. The land dipped and swayed like an old horse's back, accented by an occasional patch of trees or a sodbuster's farm. Ivory John had always hated the rolling sameness of the great plains with its incessant winds, sudden, violent storms, blowing dust and sand, and stifling summer heat. He longed for a change. *What am I doing here? Two days ago, I was on my way to the Arizona territory. I just stopped for a short visit and now my father's dead and I'm up to my neck in murder, robbery, kidnapping, and a posse of store clerks.*

As he rode, he began to think of himself as someone other than a lawman, another victim of circumstance, wronged by the brutality of men who were driven by lawlessness and greed. When they caught up with the three, he wondered if he would be able to act in a manner expected of a man wearing the badge of a US Marshal. Or would he yield to the hatred welling up in the pit of his stomach and hang the despots on the spot? He thought again of his father dying on the sidewalk in front of that pitiful little bank in the middle of nowhere. He knew well what the old sheriff thought about that badge and the oath that went with it. Could the son adhere to that same dedication to a principle held by the father under such circumstances?

"Look! Up ahead, Marshal, ain't that the Andrews girl?" one of the posse called back. "Over there, by them trees."

The riders kicked their horses to a full run and quickly reached the banker's daughter slumped like a rag doll against the trunk of a lonely tree in a small grove. She sat, unmoving, eyes staring blankly into the distance. There was no response from her as they reined-in and quickly dismounted about ten feet from her. Ivory John was the first to reach her. She was alive, but in shock. She had been savagely beaten. He knelt beside her, put his arm around her shoulder to comfort her, but she gave no response. Her body was rigid, as if she was dead. She had withdrawn deep within herself from the pain that had been forced upon her.

As the others approached, their anger began to boil over. Ivory John no longer had a posse; he now led a lynch mob. He knew he had to defuse the situation or live with the consequences. He tried to keep Missy warm with one of the two blankets he kept rolled behind his saddle.

"What're we gonna do with her while we're off catchin' those snakes?" one of the posse asked.

"Well, you are all returning to town, taking Missy safely back where she can get medical help as quickly as possible," Ivory John said.

"Not me, Marshal, I'm goin' with you to grab them jackals and string 'em up!" said another.

"No you're not! Missy Andrews needs your help more'n me. Now mount up and get goin', all of you. She needs a doctor's care in a hurry or she could die. Understand?"

"It don't take all of us to get her back home. Two could do it. The rest of us'll go with you," one of the men said as he stepped forward, incensed at the order to return to

North Platte and be denied the opportunity to be in on the kill.

"Look, I'm tellin' you, I'm goin' it alone from here on! I'll catch up to them faster by myself. Her father'd never forgive you if he figured you were more interested in killin' three hombres than helpin' his only daughter. Now, get!" Ivory John's eyes narrowed as he looked straight at the most vocal of the group. His hand fell to his side, resting on the grip of his low-slung, Colt revolver.

The men each looked around angrily to see what the others were thinking, then, murmuring among themselves as they mounted their horses, finally reached a grudging agreement that they would do as the marshal ordered.

Ivory John lifted Missy up to the arms of one of the men, stepped back and gave them a casual salute. "I'll send a telegraph when I catch 'em. They'll be comin' back for trial." He slapped the lead rider's horse on the rump.

With brief hesitation, the posse turned back toward North Platte. As he watched them go, Ivory John knew all too well what was going through the minds of those citizens. He felt a knot in his stomach, recognizing that same rage stirring within himself. He swung into the saddle and began following the clear trail that Hicks had left. *Maybe they left such an easy trail to catch me in an ambush,* he thought. *I mustn't let my hatred overcome good judgment.*

He'd not foolishly rush headlong into a trap. His father had long ago taught him the importance of not letting his heart do his thinking for him. The old man had taught him the skills of self-control that must be inherent in a man who lives by the gun. Without those skills, life can be short, indeed.

As Hicks caught up to Gar and Rufe, he let out a war whoop that made Gar turn, scowling, in his saddle. Loud noises put Gar's nerves on edge, making him even more dangerous.

"You fool, don't you know better'n than to come up on me like that? Want yer head blowed off?" Gar chastened. Then he turned away, shaking his head slowly as if to wonder what he had done to deserve a man like Hicks. After a few minutes of silence, Gar again spoke up, "Had the girl headed back to town when you got there?"

"Uh, yeah. She was gone. Probably ain't stopped runnin' yet," Hicks laughed nervously.

"You didn't touch her, did you?" Gar

raised his voice.

"Nope. I done just like you told me," Hicks said with a frown.

"Then, where'd them scratches on yer face come from?"

"I, uh, fell into a bramble tryin' to find my watch."

"You best be tellin' the truth," Gar warned, and turned back to study a crude map he held in his hand as they continued steadily toward Medicine Creek.

"Where's we headin, Gar?" Rufe finally interjected after being uncharacteristically quiet for nearly an hour.

"Colorado. Jus like you always wanted, Rufe. To see where them mountains touch the sky," Gar said, pointing to the west, as he lit a cheroot.

"Then, how come we's headin' south?" Hicks asked. "Colorado's west of here."

"Southwest. An' we'll be turnin' when I say," Gar said as he seemed to be scanning the horizon for some elusive sign.

"Whatta you keep lookin' at the sky for, Gar?" Rufe asked.

"Trouble," Gar mumbled.

"What?" Rufe and Hicks spoke together.

"Storm's comin' fast! We'll be needin' some cover, soon. Now hush up and keep kickin' them ponies."

CHAPTER EIGHTEEN

Ivory John sensed the weather was stirring up a change, and if one of those violent, plains-bred storms did come, he could easily lose the trail he was following. He was pushing the sleek black gelding as hard as he dared. If he rode too boldly, his horse might give out on him, stranding him in a most inhospitable wilderness. Properly judging his pace had become an all important factor in dogging the three desperate men, men who had no intention of making capture easy.

To the west, across rolling fields, a row of low hills in the distance drew a contrasting line between the thinning grass and the ominous beginnings of an event Ivory John had hoped he could avoid: A burgeoning thunderstorm. From the looks of what lay ahead, this thunderstorm was going to be serious. Unfortunately, shelter was a rare commodity on the plains.

The light, southerly breeze he had enjoyed for several hours was turning more westerly and increasing in intensity. The sky grew darker and darker, and he could make out flashes of lightning, streaking from the base of the angry thunderhead to the ground.

Off to the south of the trail he spotted a sodbuster's house, built with clumps of turf — Nebraska marble — stacked unevenly to make walls; grass grew from a hip-roof of short ridgepoles, willow branches, chokecherry brush and soil. A rack of elkhorns hung over the door. A corral, employing several strands of new barbed wire, was attached to the house, and two workhorses and a milk cow stood facing away from the brisk wind.

Three horses, saddled, their reins held by one imposing giant of a man, stood just outside the front door to the 'soddie.' *If these turn out to be the three I've been tracking, they must have become alarmed by the storm and swung back to the southeast, also seeking shelter.*

He couldn't approach the farmhouse without being seen by the one holding the horses, and if he stayed much longer in his present position, he'd be caught in the open by the storm. Neither option offered the kind of odds he hoped for. He needed to approach the house without anyone suspecting he was a marshal tracking three desperate men.

He thought for a moment, then decided on a plan to skirt the spread to the southeast, then come in from the south. Anyone inside would think he was just a drifter seeking shelter and be less tempted to shoot before talking. It was worth a try, and, as he started to mount the black gelding, he removed his badge and tucked it in the pocket of his black leather vest. But before he could put his plan into action, gunfire erupted from the sod house, sending two men bolting from the door toward their companion and the horses. The first man out wore a trailduster and a bowler hat. He was closely followed by a man wearing red suspenders, shooting back into the house as he exited. The three mounted quickly and rode hell-bent in the direction of the building storm.

Ivory John urged the black gelding to a full run down the hill toward the homestead. As he reined-in to a dusty halt, a badly wounded man stumbled from the doorway and collapsed on the ground in front of him. Blood covered his dirty shirt as he lay, struggling to get back on his feet. An old Sharps rifle fell from his weakened grip. The marshal dismounted and lifted the man to a sitting position, propping him up against the sod wall.

"What happened?" he asked.

The farmer blinked his eyes, trying to focus on the man who held him, his face tanned and leathery from the sun, hands gnarled from years of back-breaking work in the worthless, dusty soil he called a farm. "Three fellers . . . come a'bustin' in . . . killed my son and . . . my missus. I don't kill so easy." He struggled to get the words out, his chest heaved as he gasped for air. The front of his shirt gave clear evidence he'd been shot at close range. "Wantin' money, I-I . . . reckon."

"Who were they? Did you know them?"

"Seen a poster once . . . on the one that shot me . . . Gar Baker. The big'un was . . . his b-brother." Each difficult word brought him closer to the inevitable meeting with his maker. Ivory John could not have hoped to stop the blood gushing from the large, bubbling wound. He tried to make the man as comfortable as possible for the little time he had left. The wait would not be long.

"See to it . . . they gets . . . buried proper, and . . ." His last words ended abruptly as his head drooped slightly to one side, eyes open but empty.

"I'll see to it, mister," Ivory John whispered to the wind as he stood up and walked to the gelding, removed his hat and hung it on the pommel. He dreaded going into that dark, musty house, but he couldn't just leave those inside to the varmints. They needed burying, even though every minute that passed meant he was losing ground on the three killers. But, he had given his word. He entered the house and lifted the lifeless body of a thin woman dressed in a plain, gray cotton dress from the corner where she had sought protection behind a pine china cabinet. Two bullets had shattered the glass doors, wreaking havoc on the china plates, and exiting the back. Only one bullet found its mark, hitting the woman. By the time the piece of lead made its way through the glass, china and wood, it was so smashed out of shape, the effect was like getting hit with a sledgehammer. She died quickly.

When he caught sight of the son's body, a lad of no more than eight or nine years, tears welled up in his eyes and he had to sit outside for a spell before he could face the task of burial. The boy had been shot as he tried to hide with his mother.

These people hadn't enough food to eat let alone money to hoard, Ivory John thought. Killing for the joy of killing was something that even a marshal with Ivory John's experience seldom saw. For that he was grateful.

By the time he had finished burying the three, night had engulfed his world and the storm was upon him. He couldn't bring himself to wait out the storm in the house after what he'd seen. He decided to bed down in a drafty lean-to that served as a meager barn attached to the back of the house. He lay on the ground, propped up against his saddle, watching the awesome power that was about to overcome the dusty farm. The persistent flashes of lightning brought split-second remembrances of the brilliant midday sun, shattering the night's rightful hold on the darkness, with each flash quickly followed by an explosion of thunder. The storm raged throughout the night. By dawn, its authority had waned and it rumbled away to the northeast.

A light, cool breeze awaited Ivory John as he stirred beneath his single blanket. The sun peeked above the horizon through clear, clean air, washed and hung out to dry by the vanishing storm.

Johnson T "Ivory John" Morgan, a US Marshal at twenty-nine, had by this young age seen more action than many older peace officers in the territory. The tall, slim man with ivory-colored hair in the black pants and black vest seemed, at times, almost a magnet for trouble, attracting fools with a never-ending appetite for gunplay. Every encounter served to strengthen his resolve to help rid the frontier of the scum that preyed on the rewards of other's hard work and determination to succeed in a harsh environment. Thieves, killers, or rustlers — one was as bad as the other to Ivory John Morgan — and many a fool with a gun found out the hard way that when he came up against this quiet, young marshal, he had only two places to go: To jail or to hell, there was no in-between.

His rugged good looks and boyish smile often gave false testimony to steel nerves and a fast gun. Though he wore a perfectly balanced 1872 converted Colt .38 Navy model revolver strapped to his thigh, he actually preferred the 1873 model .44 caliber Winchester carbine which accompanied him everywhere.

"That Winchester'll get you out of more tight spots than a sidearm ever will," his father often told him. That advice had paid off more than once.

But right now, weapons were of little concern, for it appeared to Ivory John that the Baker brothers and their equally unstable partner, Dalton Hicks, had ridden directly into the jaws of the monster thunderstorm. If they hadn't stopped to seek refuge, or drowned in the flash flooding, they might have put considerable distance between themselves and any pursuers, benefiting from the storm's fury by having all traces of their trail washed away. Worse, Ivory John had not the slightest clue as to their intended destination.

Ivory John turned the slain family's livestock loose to forage on their own, then, mounting the black gelding, spurred the great animal on in the general direction he had seen the three killers strike out. After only a few miles, though, he concluded the chase had become senseless. The severity of the storm had flattened the blue grama grass and temporarily flooded vast areas with shimmering, shallow seas. The runoff would be quick, but no vestige of a trail would remain.

He decided, therefore, to ride southwest until he reached a town to send a telegraph to North Platte with the bad news. It now appeared he had failed in his pursuit. The town would have to await their revenge a bit longer.

It made little sense to ride all the way back to North Platte as his father would have been buried by then, and there was nothing left for him there. He saw as his best course of action to simply continue on toward Arizona and his new assignment. Besides, the three he sought seemed headed in the same general direction, and, with luck, he stood some chance of coming across them by persevering in that direction. He headed the gelding toward the southwest and the high mountain country.

The great storm had flushed the heat and haze from the prairie and he breathed deeply of fresh, clean air as the clouds broke. Clearing skies offered the radiant sun an opportunity to once again rule the day.

CHAPTER NINETEEN

In an attempt to put as much distance between themselves and North Platte, Gar chose to push on into the storm even as darkness overcame them. While he felt confident they had eluded any pursuers, he was a man driven not to take more chances than necessary. The storm's pounding rain provided just the kind of cover to obliterate their tracks, adding to their margin of safety.

Not everything was going well, however. Rufe rode his overburdened mount through a barbed wire fence, cutting the unfortunate animal's chest and forelegs badly. The sheer force of the horse and rider drove the flimsy fence into the muddy ground. Impatient to stop the horse's bleeding, Rufe grew angry when his horse shied away as he attempted to tend to the wounds with a salve from his saddlebags. Gar realized what was about to transpire, and grabbed his brother's massive arm just in the nick of time as the latter drew his sidearm with every intention of putting the animal down in retribution. The thought hadn't occurred to Rufe that by killing the balky horse they would then be one horse shy, thus making a rapid getaway impossible. Gar soothed the big man's anger, turning rage into reason, if only until the next time something didn't go Rufe's way.

Gar was able to calm the frightened horse and get some of Rufe's salve on the wounds. Rufe, too, seemed satisfied with the outcome. At least, for the time being.

After they'd ridden free of the storm, Gar finally gave in to Rufe's whining about needing sleep, and they stopped to make camp in a lonely stand of cottonwoods on high ground above a rain-swollen stream. Gar knew if he didn't shut Rufe up, Hicks was liable to just up and shoot him, and Gar, himself, was too weary to take on Hicks at that time. They built a small fire with the intention of bedding down for a couple of hours' sleep, feeling all the more confident that anyone tracking them would have lost their trail, as the lashing rains and swirling winds had surely destroyed any trace of their ever having passed through.

"Why'd you have to start with that sodbuster's homely woman for, anyway?" Gar said angrily, pointing an accusing finger at Hicks. "If you had just left her alone, we'd been dry and comfortable for the night, instead of near drowned in that gully-washer."

"You saw how she kept lookin' at me, like she couldn't stand bein' in the same room with me. No woman's gonna treat me like I was some sorta animal that oughta be penned up," Hicks answered through clenched teeth. Angrily, he threw a stick into the fire.

Gar's quiet frustration with Hicks simmered as he stood, leaning against a stout elm, wiping down his Colt revolver with the only dry rag he could find in his saddlebags. Finally, he was unable to keep silent any longer. Without glancing up from his task, he murmured in a deep, serious voice, "You don't have to solve every problem with that gun of yours. By shootin' her, you made me have to go and kill the other two. That sod-buster was reachin' for his Sharps. Sometimes, I figure it'd be best if we just went our different ways. Yer damned sure gonna get us all killed from all that evil you got bottled up in yer innards about women."

"If that'd set yer mind at ease, then I'll just ride on outta here!" Hicks jumped up and kicked dirt on the fire with the side of his boot. "I'm sick of bein' around that idiot brother of yours, anyhow!"

Gar stared into the flickering embers as he continued rubbing the frayed rag up and down the pistol's barrel. He was seriously considering Hick's acceptance of his spur-of-the-moment proposal. Perhaps this *would* be a good time to go their separate ways. His thoughts raced back eight months when they had come upon each other, while both were on the run from the law. It was the same day he and Rufe had held up the Omaha-Lincoln stage — where he'd blasted a man to kingdom come for trying to hang onto a gun collection, particularly the fancy Colt Peacemaker that now hung at his side — and were trying to make their trail as difficult to follow as possible by zigzagging, first to the northwest, then to the southwest, then back to the north. It was his plan to so confuse his pursuers they'd simply give up out of exhaustion. It had worked before, and Gar never quit an idea until he was proven wrong.

As the two brothers made their way over unfamiliar ground in the deep black of a moonless night, they had stumbled onto Dalton Hicks, cold camped in some underbrush with his horse staked out nearby. Gar had nearly shot the rudely awakened Hicks, mistaking him for a lawman. Only the wrinkled shirt and red suspenders convinced Gar that this man he had the drop on was not likely the law, and he held fire. Hicks was on the run for a long string of crimes. Gar suggested they ride together to confuse their hunters, and to take advantage of the additional gun.

That fateful meeting had happened back in November, and, of late, Gar had begun to regret ever asking Hicks to join him and his brother. Hicks pulled his weight on the job, when it came to robbery and general gunplay — the only form of livelihood Gar had ever known. But, because of Hicks' propensity for inflicting mayhem on women, Gar and Rufe were now included as suspects in several senseless murders of ladies.

Gar easily admitted that he, himself, was a despot, for whom morality, honesty and hard work were simply meaningless words. However, he harbored no general ill will toward anyone, man or woman. When he killed, he justified the act simply as one necessary to his survival. Hicks, on the other hand, was a cold-blooded killer, taking a life as easily as he spit tobacco juice on the ground.

Hicks' strange hatred for the opposite sex, along with his ugly temper, were fast becom-

ing a threat to the Bakers' continued survival. Gar saw the present confrontation as
an opportunity to rid himself of a liability,
probably saving Rufe's life in the bargain,
and move on to a new territory unencum-
bered.

"Yep," Gar said unemotionally, "might
just be a good time to give any that's followin' our trail somethin' to distract them.
Whittle down their numbers too. We'll take
separate trails and meet up in Denver in
two weeks. How's that set with you, Hicks?"

"Fine! Just fine! An' I'll be rid of that
simple-minded oaf for a spell too." Hicks
squatted back down on his haunches and
bit off a chew of beef jerky he'd stolen from
the sodbuster's table. He didn't really take
too favorably to the idea of riding off in different directions. If they *had* been trailed all
this time, and the posse did not split up,
there was a chance he'd be faced with fend-
ing them off alone, without benefit of Gar's
deadly Colt. On the other hand, Hicks
thought, he would be rid of Rufe, the
simpleton who grated on his nerves so
intensely. He recognized that someday, in a
fit of anger, he might have to kill Rufe, and
then he'd get to face his brother, and he
was no match for Gar Baker. They both
knew that.

Hicks took his time putting his damp bedroll together. He glanced over at Rufe sitting on a tree that had been blown down by the force of the storm. What a pathetic giant he is, he thought. His hatred of Rufe was growing. The decision to separate for awhile was well-timed.

"If we're goin' to part company, then I want my share of the spoils now," Hicks said.

"Fair enough," Gar answered, "though it ain't much, you're entitled to your share." He reached into his saddlebags and pulled out the sacks they had retrieved from the bank in North Platte. He turned each bag upside down, emptying the contents on the ground. He then sat cross-legged beside the pile and began separating the loot into three equal amounts. After several minutes of muttering over the size of the take, he said, "Well, Hicks, here's your share: One hundred and two dollars."

"You know I cain't cipher. You wouldn't hold out on me, would you, Gar?"

"I ain't never stole from my own kind, Hicks." With that said, he handed Hicks one of the bags with his share in it. Hicks grabbed it abruptly and turned on his heels, walking straight to his horse. He stuffed the small parcel in a saddlebag.

"Reckon I'll see you in Denver in a couple weeks," Hicks grumbled. He swung into the saddle and spurred his horse to a trot, heading out across the sparse grass to the west.

Gar smiled as he watched Hicks disappear over a rise, then he picked up the two remaining sacks of money and tucked them firmly into his own saddlebags. He had only cheated his partner out of a hundred or so. "C'mon, Rufe, time to get movin'."

"Where's mine?" Rufe protested.

"It'll be safer with me. Don't I always take care of you?"

"Yeah, reckon so," Rufe answered, swinging his head from side to side as he looked at the ground.

"Where is we headin', Gar?" Rufe asked as he struggled to his feet.

"Colorado! Like I been tellin' you for a week."

"Is that where that Denver place is, Gar?"

"Yes, but that's not where we're headin'."

"But that's where you told Hicks we was goin'."

"Yeh, but we're really goin' to Lake City."

"Why there?"

Drawing a wrinkled piece of paper from his pocket, Gar said, "Well, I got this here letter last year from a feller I knowed years back. He runs a gold mine for a banker back east, and he says there's ways a feller can strike it rich and never lift a hand. And that's who we're goin' to see." No more words were exchanged as the older brother stood up to break camp. Rufe frowned as he tried to comprehend what Gar had meant by striking it rich. Gar wadded the paper into a ball and threw it at the still-smoldering campfire. The letter had been written by Ezra Goode.

CHAPTER
TWENTY

As Ivory John rode, his disappointment at losing all signs of the three outlaws began to catch up to deeper emotions. He would cut the trail of the three someday, of that he was certain. Then what? Would his years of experience as a lawman translate into something that would overcome the emotional upheaval inside? He still had no answer to that nagging question.

Ivory John was starting to feel the slow-simmering pangs of vengeance rising from somewhere deep inside him. He knew these feelings could make a difference in how he would react when he came face to face with the three men who now were much more than just outlaws wanted for a far-removed crime. To survive and to achieve their capture, he would surely have to turn these personal enemies into something impersonal, simply another contact with unconscionable souls, faceless and far removed from him and his pain.

He was reminded of a lesson he'd learned as a young boy from his father. Two trail-dirty cowboys had pulled up in front of the Morgan house on the edge of town one day. They had been on their way out to rejoin their cattle drive after a couple of hours of libations at one of the many saloons in town. They had spotted a row of clean shirts and pants that hung on the clothesline, blowing gently in a warm breeze. Considering their own scruffy, dirty, and well-worn attire, they decided they had stumbled on a perfect opportunity to acquire fresh duds. As they approached, their intentions became fully obvious to Ivory John's mother, who noticed the pair through a side window. She rushed outside just as one of the men reached out to retrieve a new shirt from the line.

"What do you boys want here? Those clothes are not for sale, so you'll not be needin' to look them over," she said, standing with her hands on her hips, and looking very serious. "Best be on your way now."

"Why ma'am, we was needin' a change, and seein' as how they ain't a body usin' these duds just now, we figured we'd borry 'em for a spell. We'd bring 'em back, of course," the older of the two said with a snicker, then proceeded to yank the shirt off the line.

Mrs. Morgan nearly leaped off the porch, carrying a broomstick in a most threatening manner, making straight for the pair. "I said leave those clothes right where they are, and get!"

Young John had watched the confrontation from the house and anger welled up inside him like a spark in a dry woodpile. He decided to settle the dispute himself without further grief to his mother. He lifted an old Sharps breechloader from over the fireplace mantle and burst through the door like a miniature cavalryman to the rescue.

"You heard my ma; she said get! I'm willin' to pull this trigger if you don't get back on your horses and head out."

"Johnson, stay out of this! I can handle these two," his mother protested.

"I'm warnin' you," the boy said, ignoring his mother's admonition entirely. Raising the rifle, he took aim at the nearest cowboy.

The one holding the shirt dropped it without hesitation, but the other, less easily intimidated by a young boy, instinctively swung his hand to his sidearm and slowly began to draw it from its holster.

Just at that moment, Sheriff Morgan rounded the corner of the house on his way home for dinner. He immediately recognized the volatility of the situation, and said in a clear, stern voice, "Everybody just settle down. No need for gunplay, cowboy." The man released his grip on his six-shooter and, with a sense of relief, took two steps toward his partner, grabbed him by the arm and pulled him back.

"No harm, Sheriff," the younger cowboy stammered as he retreated for his horse. "We'll be ridin' on." Then they both hastily mounted their horses and continued down the street in the direction of their herd.

"What were you fixin' to do with that gun, son?"

"Plug those two. They were about to steal your clothes, Pa," the boy said proudly.

"Son, I'd never want to see a life lost over a shirt. Life is worth so much more than any ol' piece of cloth. If you're goin' to pick up a gun, you need to learn some priorities over its use." The sheriff took the Sharps from his son and put his arm around the boy's shoulder. "If you or your mother had been killed, I don't know what I'd have done. Listen to me, boy, and listen good. Always be sure, before you get involved in a shootout, that the punishment doesn't exceed the crime. And never let your temper draw you into a bad situation."

183

Sheriff Morgan stopped, and turned his son by the shoulders. He looked him straight in the eye, then opened the breech of the Sharps and held it up in front of the boy's face. "And another rule: Before you draw down on a body, be darned sure your weapon is loaded." Young Johnson's eyes grew as large as crabapples as he stared into the empty breech.

Ivory John smiled at the memory of his youthful impetuousness. From that day forward, lessons learned at his father's knee clung to him in everything he did, and his career as a lawman benefitted from the wisdom handed down.

He knew he must come to grips with his inner struggle. He could hear his father's words echoing in his head: *The law can be a terrible taskmaster, but must be adhered to as closely as a fly to flypaper.* Could he make a true effort to capture the three for a fair trial, or simply give in to his loathing, and shoot them before considering the actual letter of the law, making every effort to bring the outlaws in for a higher court to judge? He hoped that when the time came, he'd have sorted out his feelings. A split second of indecision could get a man killed.

Cresting a high, windblown hill, Ivory John caught sight of a barely visible, wisp of white smoke emanating from a stand of cottonwoods below and to the west, near the bank of a creek. He turned the gelding toward the trees at first, then south, following a draw to approach in such a way as to not expose himself to the camp. If it were the camp of the Bakers, a guard likely would be posted just to the right of the main group of trees, near a boulder and a clump of shrubs. He could avoid being spotted by staying low and close to the westernmost edge of the draw. Within a hundred yards or so of the trees, he dismounted, tied the gelding loosely to a fingery limb jutting from the earthen wall, and proceeded on foot, cautiously using the plentiful scrub brush as cover, to within a few feet of the thin ribbon of smoke.

The camp was abandoned, but the fire had not been completely smothered. Whoever had camped there had been in a big hurry to leave. Fresh tracks marked the soft ground around where the fire had been. The camp had been made after the storm, and abandoned only a few hours before he arrived. He slipped into the camp and carefully probed the area around the few still smoldering embers for clues. A cloth bag from the North Platte Settler's Bank lay in plain view. Ivory John knew he had stumbled onto the camp of his father's murderers.

He could clearly see their trails splitting off in two different directions from the campsite. Two horses headed off to the southwest, and the third struck out on a more westerly course. Without a posse to split up into two groups, he had to go it alone. Which trail should he follow?

He stood stroking his bushy mustache and pondering his best course of action when a wadded-up piece of paper, lying near the edge of some half-burned sticks, caught his eye. He realized it must have been intended for the fire but had fallen short and had merely been singed. There was enough writing still legible to reveal much about its owner and to make his decision as to which trail to follow. The letter had been written by a man named Ezra and sent to Gar Baker. It suggested he and his brother should come to Lake City, Colorado where the pickin's were good for his kind of profession.

With the clear tracks of two horses leading off to the southwest, in the general direction of Lake City, Ivory John now knew where to find Gar and Rufe. That left him free to follow the single trail of the third man, Dalton Hicks. That was fine with Ivory John, since he figured all along that Dalton

Hicks was most likely the one to have beaten Missy Andrews. It couldn't have been either of the Baker brothers, he reasoned, as they never left each other's side, and he'd found only one set of tracks left by Missy's attacker. Besides, Hicks was the one with the reputation for often fatal mayhem toward women, a reputation he'd earned long before joining the Bakers.

Ivory John wanted Hicks almost more than the other two. His hatred for the man was intense. And he was burning with a desire to see justice done on Missy's behalf, even if it came at the point of a bullet.

Ivory John mounted the black gelding and began to follow the single trail west.

CHAPTER
TWENTY-ONE

Dalton Hicks rode without hurry. After breaking off from the Baker brothers, he decided at first to follow Frenchman Creek, cut southwest for Fort Morgan, then head straight to Denver for their rendezvous. He saw no need to waste his horse by running him to death. He was confident that the storm had obliterated his trail. There had been no sign of anyone on their trail since they rode out of North Platte. And besides, while he was relieved to be free of Rufe Baker for a while, a plan was beginning to come together for him, a plan that would accomplish something he'd been thinking about ever since he hooked up with the Baker brothers. From the moment he first saw it, he'd wanted to get his hands on that gleaming, nickel-plated Colt Peacemaker that Gar wore so proudly. That gun was more than just a weapon, it had a personality, it got attention, and it was going to be his one way or another, even if he had to kill to get it. That's the only reason he planned to join back up with Gar and his idiot brother in Denver.

Hicks knew the money he had received as his share of the ill-fated bank robbery wasn't going to take him very far. He was on the lookout for a way to enhance his poke. That opportunity came two days later in the form of a small settlement called Oak Prairie, along the banks of Frenchman Creek. He stumbled onto the little community just before he was to cross into Colorado. The town was insignificant in its collection of small wooden buildings and tents, quickly constructed to provide goods and services to the growing farm community. But the creek had overflowed its banks so often from the plentiful spring rains, its citizens had grave doubts about the town's long-term survival. Many had already moved downstream to higher ground in anticipation of building something more substantial. Small as it was, the town held sufficient prospect to Hicks for lifting a few dollars toward his continued journey west. As he rode in, he decided to stay around long enough to identify a target. It was not long in coming.

The settlement did have a bank. The hastily built, yet unfinished wooden structure seemed too easy for Hicks to pass up. He went to the livery stable to bed down his horse. Then he ventured out to acquaint himself with some of the citizenry who were gathered in a tent that served as one of the town's two saloons.

"Howdy, name's Smith," Hicks said as he moved up to a long table that sufficed as the bar. The man next to him turned, smiled, and then nodded before tossing back a shot of whiskey.

The man placed the glass on the bar, requested another, then said, "I'm Mordecai Long, pleased to meet you. What brings you to Oak Prairie, Mr. Smith?"

"Just passin' through," Hicks responded. "Plan to be here a couple of days. You folks got someplace a feller can put a hunnert dollars or so for safe keepin'?"

"The Oak Prairie Bank's as safe as any, I reckon. Only got a strongbox, though. New safe's comin' next week from St. Louis. A real sturdy one. Then, there won't be any question where's the safest place for a body's valuables," Mordecai said.

Hicks ordered a whiskey for himself and another for Mordecai. They talked for nearly half an hour, then Hicks left to bed down at the stable. The talkative old man had informed him that the sheriff had ridden over to Fort Wallace with a prisoner, an Indian who'd gotten drunk and shot a farmer. Since the Army had jurisdiction over the Indians, the sheriff was obliged to deliver his prisoner to the fort for trial. Hicks was already counting his money as he threw a blanket down on a bed of straw next to his saddle and lay back with a greedy smile on his face.

The next morning, he awoke with a desire to get the robbery over with as soon as possible. He'd learned more than enough from old Mordecai to proceed without further need to study the layout. He'd have breakfast at the tent restaurant down the street, then saddle his horse, walk him to the bank and tie him out back. It was Sunday; there'd be no one inside to put up a fight. He'd just break the lock off the back door and walk in. Simple.

After breakfast, he strolled nonchalantly while leading his horse down the street to the bank. Nearly everyone in town was gathered in a simple one-room building that served as the town's only church. As he passed it, he paused briefly to scoff at the familiar strains of a hymn he remembered his hated stepmother singing as he was growing up. Then, he continued around to the rear of the bank. At the back door, he picked up a large, jagged rock and brought it down hard on the flimsy padlock that secured the plank door. One well-placed blow tore the hinge out of the soft wood. Hicks slipped into the bank unnoticed.

Behind a counter sat the strongbox, wrapped in chains held in place with two more padlocks, stronger than the one on the door, and too strong for breaking with a rock. *I'll have to shoot these off, gather the money in those two pouches on the table, and ride out of here before anyone can figure out what's happened,* he thought. He drew his sidearm, and took aim at the first lock. It released its grip as the single shot shattered the case. He quickly took aim at the other and fired. The result was the same. He yanked the chains from around the reinforced box and pried open the latch with his boot knife. Inside, a surprise greeted him. There was no more than fifty dollars in the strongbox, along with a few baubles of jewelry and a small bundle of bonds wrapped with twine.

"What the hell is this? Even the damned banks don't have money no more!" he muttered through clenched teeth. He hastily stuffed the few bills into his pocket, then turned to escape through the back door. As he reached the door, Hicks saw several armed men approaching from the alley behind the bank. The townsfolk had responded to the sound of his shooting off the locks much faster than he anticipated. It looked like he had misjudged this small, sleepy village. He bolted to the front door and spotted more armed men racing up the street toward the bank. He drew his gun and fired through the glass pane of the door, mortally wounding one of the surprised oncomers. Turning to check on the men out back, he found two of them coming on fast. He fired two shots through the open back door, killing them both on the spot.

Eight men had answered the alarm sounded by a citizen who was passing the bank at the same time Hicks fired the first shot to break into the strongbox. The remaining five scattered and ran for cover. Realizing they had more than a mere robber on their hands, and no sheriff to lead them, the men became less than anxious to risk getting shot by this accomplished marksman. Occasionally, one would throw a shot into the bank building from across the street, but none dared venture very far from his safe refuge behind a barrel, building, or watering trough. For the time being, at least, both sides would await the other's next move.

Hicks couldn't get out and the townsfolk couldn't get in, and that situation didn't set well with the impatient outlaw. He needed a plan to extricate himself from the bank. He didn't like the idea that he could be rushed from both sides. He felt trapped. He took up a position crouching behind the bank counter. From there he could keep an eye on both the front and rear doors. Hicks decided that if he could just reach his horse, he might be able to make it to the livery stable, where he could make a better stand from the loft. From there, he could hold off anyone until nightfall. Then he would set fire to the building. While the townsfolk dashed about, trying to get nearby buildings wetted down sufficiently to avoid a conflagration, he'd simply ride out through the confusion.

The plan had its disadvantages, since he couldn't count on the defenders to stay put and do nothing, but he figured these farmers wouldn't risk their lives so easily after seeing three of their own go down. He eased his way toward the back door. As he reached the open door, he swallowed hard at the sight before him: His horse lay dead in the alley, struck by a stray bullet. Making it to the livery on foot without some sort of diversion was a long shot at best, but his present position was becoming more untenable by the minute. He had to make a move.

Ivory John rode into the outskirts of Oak Prairie just as the shooting at the bank began. He stopped in front of the empty sheriff's office and dismounted. Spotting the glint of sunlight off the marshal's badge, Mordecai Long ran to him from across the street.

"You're a lawman, ain't you?" he called.

"US Marshal."

"Then, we'll be needin' your help, Marshal," Mordecai said. "There's a robber holed up in the bank down to the other end of town, and the sheriff's off to Fort Wallace with that Injun that shot Lem Duncan."

"Slow down, old timer, and tell me what's happened," Ivory John asked as he tied his gelding to the hitching rail and pulled his Winchester from the saddle boot.

"Rode in yesterday, started askin' questions about a safe place to put his money, and . . ."

"Do you know who this man is?"

"Didn't then, do now!" Mordecai reached into his pocket, pulled out a folded piece of paper, and held it in front of the marshal.

195

"That's him. After the shootin' started, I went to the sheriff's office and pulled this off the wall. Knowed I'd seen him someplace before."

"That's the man I'm after: Dalton Hicks. Head me toward that bank, friend," Ivory John said, motioning for the man to lead the way.

As they approached the bank, the marshal saw how the town had Hicks pretty well bottled up, but had no way of getting to him without significant casualties. He stayed out of sight of the bank's front window, so Hicks wouldn't spot a lawman. He figured Hicks had tried such a stupidly bold robbery mainly because he knew the sheriff was away, assuming the town had been left without protection. Ivory John wanted to let that assumption stand for a few minutes longer.

From a short distance away, two farmboys in town for supplies overheard the conversation between Ivory John and Mordecai Long.

"Did you hear that, Bob? That's Dalton Hicks holed up in the bank. I seen a poster on him hangin' outside the sheriff's office. He's worth five hundred," the oldest one whispered. He took his brother by the arm and pulled him out of earshot of the marshal.

"What're you thinkin', Jed? I've seen that look on yer face before." Bob brushed a lock of blond hair out of his eyes. He squinted at his brother with suspicion.

"I'm thinkin' that money could be ours."

"How do you figure that?"

"By us takin' that outlaw before the marshal can get to him, that's how," Jed said proudly. He tugged at his younger brother's sleeve, pulling him into the shadows beside Larson's General Store.

Bob reluctantly followed, weakly pulling against his brother's grip as his only protest. "Jed, that man in there is a killer. The only thing we ever killed was rabbits."

"Then that's what we'll do. We'll flush him out just like a rabbit. Then we got him."

"I don't like it! We could get ourselves killed! This ain't nothin' like flushin' no rabbit."

"Would be with the proper tools."

"What tools you talkin' about, Jed?" Bob asked, taking a step away, toward the street. Bob had been drawn into foolish actions more than once before by his older brother. Each time he swore he'd learned his lesson. But, then, there'd never been $500 at stake before. He thrust his hands through the bib

197

of his overalls, stared at the ground, and drew a line in the dirt with the toe of his badly worn shoe.

"What'd we just pick up at Larson's?" Jed prompted.

"Uh . . . beans, canned goods, an ax handle . . . and dynamite."

"That's gonna be our tool!"

"What?"

"The dynamite!"

"Are you crazy? Pa would skin us if we took his dynamite! How's he gonna blow stumps out back if we use it up?"

"We'll only need two sticks. An' besides, with the reward money, we can buy Pa all the dynamite in the county. You with me?" Jed started for the wagon without waiting for an answer.

"I-I don't know. How're you gonna use that stuff?" Bob asked, trailing along behind. Jed often had inventive ideas about how the two could make some quick money. The older brother had always wanted to go east to St. Louis and see the fancy houses along tree-lined streets like he'd seen in the *Harper's* newspaper at Larson's. He never acted on his ideas, however, mainly because they always seemed to require work, and Jed was fed up with work. Living on a farm had brought him all the work he wanted.

This time, Jed's idea seemed to be shaping up differently, and Bob was concerned that his nineteen-year-old brother was going to go through with it. He wondered if, in two years when he'd be nineteen, he'd be driven by stupid ideas too.

Jed pried the lid off the wooden box of dynamite sticks. A smaller box of coiled fuse and detonator caps sat nearby. He held up two sticks of the explosive, and tied them together with a string. A length of fuse stuck into a detonator cap curled out of the middle of the bundle. He handed the dynamite to Bob.

"Now, what you do is light this here fuse, run across the street, and toss the whole thing through that broken door glass. When ol' Hicks sees what's about to happen — his goin' to be blown to smithereens and all — he'll be headin' out that back door lickety-split. That's when I capture him, dead or alive, just like the poster says." Jed held his tongue between his teeth as he finished tying the final knot on the bundle of explosives in Bob's hands.

Bob stared wide-eyed, mouth agape at Jed. His brother had completely lost his mind. "What if he shoots *me,* instead?" Bob asked with a catch in his voice.

"There's no way he can hit you when

you're runnin', dummy! Just stay low." Jed dug down in his pocket, secured a tin of matches, fished one out and handed it to Bob.

"Where are you gonna be?"

"Out back of the bank. I'll be ready for him."

"Wh-what if he comes out and you have to shoot him and that ol' Sharps misfires like she's done before?"

"Will you quit soundin' like Ma? Ain't nothin' goin' to happen, except that we're gonna collect us five hundred dollars. That's for sure."

Bob stood rocking back and forth against the wagon's tailgate. "I-I don't really like this idea, Jed."

"You ain't gonna pull up lame on me are you?"

"Well —"

"Course you ain't. Now, give me five minutes to get in position, then get goin'. I'll be ready and waitin'," Jed said as he lifted the Sharps from beneath the seat of the wagon, then sprinted toward the alley.

Bob nervously rolled the match between his fingers. He tried to count out five minutes under his breath.

CHAPTER
TWENTY-TWO

Ivory John was intent on extracting as much information concerning the layout of the bank building as the old man could provide. "How many ways in, Mordecai?"

"Well, there's the front door near the north end, a back door dead center off the alley, and I reckon you might get in from the balcony through one of them upper windows. Of course that creaky ol' floor'd probably give you away."

"Rotten layout," the marshal grumbled. "Need to get him outta there. Where does that alley go?"

"Goin' north, it opens out onto Front Street, up there by the dry goods store. The other end comes out south, there at the livery and corral. Why?" Mordecai asked with a puzzled look.

"I'll need the help of some of the citizens, if they're willin'."

"We stick together around here. You can

count on us, Marshal."

"Good. Here's what I want you to do. Leave two men to cover the doors, one across the street, and one out back. Tell them to keep tossin' lead into the building to keep Hicks busy. Call the rest together for a meetin' over there beside that little dress shop, out of sight of the bank. I'll tell everyone the plan when we meet. Any questions?"

"No sir."

"Then get goin', we don't have much time to put this thing into action."

Within minutes, several men had gathered around the marshal, talking among themselves about putting an end to a bank robber's career, and how Hicks would have done well to have picked someplace more tolerant of his kind than Oak Prairie.

Five minutes were up. The time for Bob to move was at hand. He noticed the men moving away from their positions around the bank building, but gave it no thought as he drew the match across the heel of his shoe, touched the flame to the thirty-second fuse, then rushed into the street toward the bank.

When the man covering the front of the building saw Bob racing directly into his line of fire, he ceased shooting for fear of hitting the boy.

Just as he reached the step up to the boardwalk, Bob stumbled and fell, fumbling the explosive as he went down. The bundle tumbled end over end as it flew through the air. The dynamite had no more than bounced off the door of the bank when it exploded with a deafening roar, harmlessly showering the street, and Bob, with splinters of wood and dirt.

Inside, huddled behind the heavy oak counter, Hicks went unscathed by the blast. He instantly saw it as an opportunity to make good his escape out the back door. Through the dirt, smoke and confusion, he darted from the open door, firing as he went. He fired at anything that moved or even looked like it might.

Jed sprang from his hiding place behind a rain barrel, but before he could bring the balky old Sharps to bear on his target, a well-aimed bullet from Hick's Remington slammed into the boy's forehead. Jed slumped back in his position behind the barrel, stone dead. The man assigned to cover the back entrance lay cowering on the ground behind the dead horse, fearful of becoming the next target of that deadly .44.

Hicks raced south down the alley toward the corral, a horse, and freedom. Things had gone more smoothly when he was riding with Gar Baker, he thought, even with having to suffer the presence of that imbecile, Rufe.

Nearly out of breath as he reached the locked door to Central Livery and Corral, he wasted no time in shooting off the padlock. Once inside, the seriousness of his growing dilemma became evident. He was nearing panic as he made his next discovery: There were no horses! It would be two or three minutes at most before those men who had kept him at bay for so long made their way to him, and he was almost out of ammunition.

"Where are all the damned horses?" he shouted in frustration, running from stall to stall as if there might just be one hidden somewhere he couldn't see. For all his hoping, nothing changed in his favor.

"Don't make any sudden moves or you're a dead man, Hicks," Ivory John called from just inside the open door. He had slipped into the stable unnoticed as the outlaw stumbled about in desperation.

Startled by the voice behind him, Hicks whirled around to find himself staring at a lanky marshal aiming a Winchester at him.

Hicks fired wildly as he dove for cover in a stall.

"I'm takin' you in for murder, mister," the marshal said, as Hicks' shot went wide. The marshal quickly moved aside to use a large vertical beam for cover.

"Murderin' who?" Hicks called nervously, his eyes darting about for some means of escape. His hand gripped the Remington tightly as he appraised his situation.

"For starters, the sheriff back in North Platte. Then there was that farm family west of Medicine Creek. And how about those two lyin' out there in the alley?"

"I didn't kill that sheriff, Gar done that."

"And lastly, for what you did to that young girl you took from the bank in North Platte, beating her senseless."

"That homely little thing treated me like dirt. Ain't nobody can get away with that." Hicks snickered to himself as he remembered Missy Andrews, and how she kinda reminded him of his dead stepmother.

Enough of looking back, he thought. He had to set his mind to the task at hand. He was in a jam, and he knew he'd have to make his move soon or chances were the young man behind that badge and rifle would make it for him. Facing a man experienced with a gun wasn't Hicks' idea of good odds, and right then he wished Gar had been there with that lethal Colt Peacemaker, instead of the heavy old Remington. But fate had dealt him a different hand, and it was time to bet or fold, shoot or get shot.

Ivory John held the Winchester at the ready. He knew a fool like Dalton Hicks wasn't going to give up without a fight. It wasn't looking good for any kind of easy arrest, and that was all right with the marshal. This man was going to make a desperate move, he could feel it. So Ivory John decided to make it as easy as possible for the outlaw. Hicks' reputation was as a good shot, but not a fast gun. The odds favored the marshal and his rifle. He waited. He had chambered a round and left the rifle cocked before entering the building, and he had yet to fire a shot.

"Throw out that sidearm, Hicks, or face the consequences."

"What'll you do, Marshal, shoot me down? You ever kill a man before, *kid?*" Hicks goaded, judging that a marshal that young must also be inexperienced.

Ivory John made no reply. He stood motionless, ready for whatever strategy Hicks was about to set into motion.

"That's it, ain't it? You ain't never shot no one before and you're scared. Scared yellow. What's your name, Marshal? They'll need to know for your tombstone," Hicks laughed. "And besides, I like to know a body's name before I blow a hole in his skull." He gripped the revolver tightly with the hammer cocked. His confidence was building as he assessed his opponent to be a green lawman. The time seemed right to add just such a man to his list of killings.

"Morgan. Some call me Ivory John."

Hicks had already stepped quickly from behind the protection of the heavy slats in the stall when he realized his error in judgment. The man he faced was no "green" lawman. Indeed, Ivory John Morgan had a reputation for consistently bringing his quarry back, dead or alive — often, more dead than otherwise.

Ivory John aimed to bring Hicks down, not to kill him, as he wheeled around from behind the large support he'd sought refuge behind. The young marshal's skill with the Winchester became evident in the blink of an eye and a burst of fire. His bullet smashed through Hicks' gun arm before the outlaw could get a shot off, shattering his elbow and spinning him to the ground. Hicks struggled to his knees, cradling his bloody arm and screaming.

"Don't shoot no more, Marshal, I'm

done!" Hicks cried. "Get me a doc, I'm hurt bad. You near blowed my arm clean off!"

"You'll live. Now get to your feet, you're on your way back to North Platte to hang," Ivory John said through clenched teeth. He reached down and grabbed Hicks by the collar and pulled him to his feet. He had no sympathy for the wounded man's pain considering all the people who'd suffered at his hands.

As they came from the dark barn into the sunlight, several armed men approached.

"Good job, Marshal."

"Looks like he'll need a little patchin' up. I'll get Doc."

"We'll take him to the jail for you, Marshal," Mordecai offered as he caught up to them. Ivory John nodded as he stepped back to let two men lead Hicks off. He followed several steps behind with Mordecai.

Even through the stabbing pain of his shattered right arm, Hicks knew if they got him into that cell, it was all over for him. His mind raced to come up with an escape plan before they covered the two blocks to his imminent incarceration. It came as he looked over at one of the men walking alongside him.

Just before reaching the door to the jail, Hicks, using his good left hand, made a desperate grab for the six-gun of the man on his left. Success! He spun away, thumbed back the hammer of the gun he held shakily in his left hand. He pointed it at his two escorts.

"Stand back or you're both dead," he growled.

From across the street, a figure emerged out of the shadows, raised an old Sharps rifle and fired. A loud crack and a puff of white smoke belched from the barrel of the old weapon. Hicks fell backward to a dusty end. His hasty attempt at freedom was to be his last.

Dalton Hicks lay sprawled in the street, dead eyes open wide in disbelief. Young Bob's single shot from the Sharps had caught the outlaw squarely in the chest, killing him almost instantly. Bob dropped the rifle into the street and fell to his knees in tears.

As Ivory John stepped into the surprised group of men, people came running from all over to hover over the remains of the man who had coveted their paltry savings.

Mordecai was the first to speak. "We're grateful you was around when we needed you, Marshal. Thanks. Don't worry none about the boy, he'll be alright. This man just murdered his brother, he figured he had the right."

Ivory John nodded as he walked to his horse and replaced the rifle in the saddle boot.

He wouldn't spend any sleepless nights over the events of that day. Vengeance, when the critical time came, had given way to calm reason. He had given Dalton Hicks every chance to give up peaceably. The outlaw would have surely hanged, though not without a fair trial. But, now that fate, in the guise of a young farmboy, had taken Dalton Hicks' judgment out of the hands of any earthly court, Ivory John was satisfied that the punishment had, indeed, fit the crime.

"Where are you headed, now?" the old man questioned.

"Colorado. I'm hopin' to meet up with that fella's partners. We got unfinished business. This town have a telegraph office?"

"Sure," answered Mordecai.

The marshal pulled a scrap of paper from his vest pocket and the stub of a pencil from his saddlebag. He tore the paper in half, then scratched a few words on each and handed them to the old man. "Send this one to the mayor of North Platte, he'll be wantin' to know about what's just happened. Then, send the other to the sheriff of

Lake City, Colorado."

Mordecai took the messages and hurried down the street as Ivory John mounted the black gelding and pointed him toward the high country.

CHAPTER
TWENTY-THREE

July, 1878

Having been born and raised on the rolling farmlands of the prairie, the Baker brothers discovered making their way through the rugged Rocky Mountains was an unexpectedly difficult experience. The way was arduous and fraught with danger nearly every step of the way.

Gar scowled at Rufe as he said, "I'm damn sick of these mountains. A man can't ride in a straight line for more'n a few minutes." He swatted wildly at the millionth black fly to attack him that day.

"What'll we do, Gar? Where'll we go? Can we go home, now? Can we, huh?" A confused, pathetic look came over the sweaty giant as he twisted uneasily in his saddle.

"Shut up, you idiot! We ain't got a home, but if you wanna leave, then GO!"

"But, Gar, I can't go nowhere without you." The sudden realization that his brother might leave him to fend for himself brought a momentary rush of desperation to Rufe as he wiped his brow with the back of his dirty hand.

The truth of Rufe's statement burnt deep into Gar's thoughts. He couldn't leave his imbecile brother alone, even for a day. He was fully aware that Rufe, if deserted, was capable of near maniacal fits of anger, with the capacity to kill every living thing in sight, and even Gar Baker wanted nothing to do with loosing that kind of terror on the countryside. He had once thought of killing Rufe. But, from somewhere in the dark reaches of his mind, his dead mother's voice screeched, admonishing him for such a thought, condemning him to hell forever if he should actually go through with it. That vivid memory was the only thing that stood between Rufe's living and dying on more than one occasion. Gar Baker was forever saddled with his maladroit sibling, and that was that.

One week of steady riding had put them well into the high mountain country and the uncertainty of which trails to follow. Often no trail was evident and they simply followed the path of least resistance until it put them in a box canyon or atop a sheer cliff with no possibility of further progress, and, time after time, they'd backtrack to try yet another recourse.

Yet, the promise of wealth without effort drove Gar willingly to suffer the hardship of the landslides, flash floods and mountain lions on the prowl around their camp at night. Even Rufe was placated by assurances of riches beyond imagination, and lulled into acceptance of his temporary adversity. And, so, they pushed on toward Lake City, and the lure of gold.

Sheriff John C. Tauber was startled from a light snooze while sitting at his desk — a ritual indulged in every afternoon about the same time — by Jeffrey Eliot, the town telegrapher. "Got a telegram for you, Sheriff. It sounds important."

"Just read it to me, I'm too tired to put on my readin' glasses," the sheriff said, scooting down even lower in his chair, feet braced against an open drawer.

"It says, 'Be on lookout for Gar and Rufe Baker. Wanted for murder and robbery in Nebraska. Thought to be headed your way. Johnson T Morgan, US Marshal.' Want I should send any kind of reply?"

"What kind of reply would you send, Jeffrey?" The sheriff lifted one eyebrow questioningly. "Have you seen any strangers in town that might be them two?"

"Uh, well, no . . . I reckon not."

"Well, just leave the paper there on the desk and I'll get back to you if there's a change in that."

"Okay, Sheriff," the man said, and turned to scurry back through the front door. Sheriff Tauber twisted around in his chair to reach for a stack of wanted posters piled on a table behind him. He shuffled through them twice, then replaced them as they had been. Nothing here on those two, he thought, reckon we'll just wait and see what happens. He yawned, then stretched, and slowly strolled out into the afternoon sun for a reassuring look at what had seemingly become a very peaceful town, a town he had played a large part in settling down.

He thought of that day, nearly a year back, when Johnny Beaver had saved his life by shooting Ezra Goode before Goode could get a clean shot off at the sheriff, caught in the open on the narrow path leading up to the abandoned mine shaft. He remembered the ill-starred nickel-plated Colt Peacemaker that had resided for a time in his desk drawer, turned in by young Johnny after the shooting, wanting nothing to do with guns again. And whatever happened to that fancy Colt? Was it now in the possession of someone with better judgment than its first owner, Creeg Bedloe? He could only hope.

He decided it wouldn't hurt to do a little follow-up on the telegram. He stepped into the street and casually started for the Little Nugget Saloon. He would cover all the saloons in Lake City that day, asking each bartender to be on the lookout for two strangers, requesting each to let him know if anyone unfamiliar to them should appear troublesome. Bartenders were often the first to know anything worthy of note that happened in town.

"Hold up here," said Gar, as he casually raised his hand, "that may be the mine over there, halfway up that rise, yonder."

"Don't appear to be much," Rufe grumbled. "Look how the sign's fallen down and everythin's turned to rust."

"Don't look like much for sure, but Ezra'd tell it true, so must be he don't want a body snoopin' around. We'll ride up closer and see for ourselves."

"Okay, Gar," Rufe said, clucking his tongue to get his weary horse to move.

They followed a rock-strewn trail to the mine entrance where they stopped. Just as Gar started to dismount, he heard the sound of a gun being cocked.

"Stay where you are, mister, and git them hands in the air. This ain't no place for nosy strangers. You're standin' on my claim and I'll shoot the first one of you that even looks like he thinks different." The gravelly voice had come from behind some boulders near the mine entrance.

"Now just hold on, we ain't come to rob you nor nothin'. We're just be lookin' for Ezra Goode. Is that you?" Gar asked.

"Nope. He ain't around," came the answer.

"Know where he could be found? He told me to come in a letter he done wrote awhile back," Gar said. The brothers sat, unmoving, with hands in the air as instructed, although Gar's eyes darted about, seeking to identify exactly where the unfamiliar voice was coming from in case they had to fight their way out of the situation.

"Ol' Ezra couldn't write. I done all his writin' for him. What's your name?"

"Gar Baker, down from Nebraska." Gar threw a thumb over his shoulder in the general direction of east. "This here's my brother, Rufe."

With the sound of rocks dribbling down the hard-packed soil, a crusty old man appeared from behind a boulder, holding a Colt Army revolver in his hand. He eyed them both for a bit, then holstered his weapon and motioned for the two to dismount. "I remember that letter. Reckon that'd be about a year back. Ezra's been gone near that long. Come on in and sit a spell, gents. Name's Benson — me and Ezra was friends for years before his gettin' hisself shot and all."

Rufe clumsily slid off his horse, nearly slipping and falling on the slickrock that covered the ground around him. Gar followed Benson into the entrance of the mine, where rubble and pieces of old crates littered a small, dug out room. They each picked a rickety crate and sat. Rufe's nearly collapsed from his weight.

Benson pulled a small bag of tobacco from his shirt pocket and held it out to Gar. "Smoke?" he asked. Rufe reached for the bag and Gar promptly slapped the big man's hand like a mother slapping a child for reaching into the cookie jar. Rufe quickly pulled his hand back, rubbing it and frowning.

"Rufe don't smoke, he chokes," Gar said, shooting Rufe a sideways frown. "So, what happened that Ezra got hisself shot?"

"They say he killed the owner of this mine, a feller from back east, then he stabbed ol' Simon Stover, the livery owner, and stole his stash. If you was to ask me, I'd say it was that damned breed that done Stover. Anyway, the sheriff tracked Ezra to the mountains south of here, and they shot him. He never got no chance to tell his side, nor nothin'."

"Did Ezra shoot the mine owner?"

"Welll . . . maybe he did that, but he was sure to have his reasons." Benson cradled his rough, unshaven chin in his hand and sighed. "I been keepin' a lookout on things here for the past few months."

"Find any gold?" Gar asked.

"Only a mite. Mostly this here mine's played out. Barely enough to keep a soul from starvin'."

The room was wet and stuffy; the air humid and still. Gar sat silently for a few minutes, then stood up and walked outside.

"Where's he goin'?" Benson asked.

"He's thinkin'," Rufe said with the innocence of a child.

Benson got slowly to his feet and shuffled off after Gar, leaving Rufe alone to glance about nervously in the cool, musty, near-dark surroundings. Beads of sweat broke out on Rufe's forehead as his bulging eyes searched about, trying to identify the source of scurrying sounds coming from deep back in the shaft. With a shudder, he suddenly clambered to his feet and burst out of the mine entrance into the stifling heat. The sun beat down with the intensity of a fiery avalanche. He blinked repeatedly to get his eyes adjusted to the brightness. He noticed Gar and Benson standing in a shady spot near the horses, talking lowly. He took several deep breaths, then, being careful not to fall as he crossed the shale pile, sat on a rock near his horse and mopped his brow with a dirty, wrinkled handkerchief fished out of his hip pocket.

"The letter said a man could make a fortune here and hardly turn a hand. How can that be, ol' man, since you're barely keepin' alive? Did Ezra take some sorta secret with him to the grave?" Gar asked.

"No secret, just that now he's dead, ain't nobody to head up the operation."

"Operation? What operation?"

"Long before the owner, ol' Duckworth, arrived in town, Ezra knowed this hole was dried up, that his days was numbered, so, he conjured up a plan to relieve some of the other miners in the area of their excess weight."

"What was the plan?"

"There's a heap of claim jumpin' and stealin' goin' on around here. And, there ain't enough law to put a stop to it. So, Ezra figured he'd get together some rough types and form a safety committee, offer protection to the other miners, for a nice big cut, of course." Benson grinned toothlessly.

"Think it'd work?" Gar asked.

"Might, if the right man was to take the reins. A man that'd make 'em see they didn't have no choice. You interested?"

"Might be. Where would we git these other men?"

"Reckon I could round up a half dozen or so here'bouts."

"Do it, then. My brother and I'll ride on into town to size up the law. We'll be meetin' you back here in two days. Okay?"

Benson turned without saying a word, just gave a wave as he disappeared back into the mouth of the mine. Gar whistled for Rufe to get to his horse as he mounted his own.

"We'll be goin' into town, little brother. Get your mouth set for a big ol' steak," Gar said as he looked back over his shoulder at Rufe, who was grinning like he'd just opened a fancy present.

CHAPTER
TWENTY-FOUR

The rugged, sometimes trail meandered and dodged around boulders, granite cliffs and numerous blow-downs; across rocky streams that seemed to appear abruptly out of nowhere, wallow around over a stony bed, then disappear as quickly into a sink hole or cave; climbing through thick, pine forests that scratched welts on a man's arms, and over stretches of barren sand that could support only snakes and lizards.

Ivory John grew tired of the barely discernible pathway through the high mountains, and he often let the black gelding pick his own way through long stretches of trail, trusting the horse's better sense of the unknown. He thus allowed his mind to wander over the events of the past weeks, trying to ignore his surroundings. It was just one such lapse that nearly cost him his life.

After crossing a shallow stream, his horse started up a rocky bank, passing below an outcropping of monolithic boulders over which hung a crown of trees, bent and bowed from winters of fifteen-foot snowfalls that served to keep them humble. The quiet was shattered by a sudden, blood-curdling scream from above. Startled, the gelding shied, then reared up on his hind legs, dislodging a surprised Ivory John who rolled over the horse's rump to land in an unmanly heap on the moist ground. Before the marshal could gather his wits, a large mountain lion crashed through the high brush and fell dead at his feet, followed a split second later by the unmistakable sound of a rifle echoing off the canyon walls, originating from some distance away. The well-aimed bullet had hit the lion cleanly through the heart, killing him midleap, a leap intended to unseat the barely awake marshal with a killing blow from razor-sharp claws and two hundred pounds of momentum.

"Damn!" was all Ivory John could manage to sputter as he struggled to his feet, brushing dirt and leaves off himself. "I'll be damned," he repeated as he stood over the beautiful, still beast. He ran a shaky hand through his dust-matted hair, then replaced his Stetson on his head.

Just then, he heard the sound of something

— man or beast he couldn't tell — crashing heavily through the brush near the trail just ahead. His rifle was still booted on his horse, now some thirty feet away. He drew his revolver from the tied-down holster in preparation for whatever or whoever was about to burst through the thicket beside the trail. He raised the revolver, ready to fire at first recognition of threat to his life. Then, suddenly, something hairy and large — something he first took for a bear — erupted in an explosion of leaves and broken twigs, stopping abruptly in front of him some ten feet away at the edge of the clearing. It was a very large, bearded man, dressed quite strangely for a hot summer day in a shaggy buffalo coat and a floppy brimmed hat. The man clutched a Henry rifle in his right hand.

"Damn, I near shot when I heard you come a'stompin' through the underbrush like a stampedin' bull," Ivory John blurted out, half angrily. He holstered his Colt, pulling a face.

"Obliged you didn't, friend. I just come down to collect ol' Devil's hide." The man strode quickly across the clearing and knelt down beside the fallen animal. He pulled out a large bowie knife, and commenced to slit the animal down its belly. "Been trackin' him for almost ten miles. He jumped a trapper up yonder, near that ridge," he said, pointing a bloody blade in the direction from which he had just come. "Killed the poor man and started to feed on him. They don't usually go near man unless they're trapped or wounded, but once they taste human flesh, well, they'll track a man down. Reckon you just come up on his list of meal choices."

"So it appears. Much obliged, mister, for some mighty fine shootin'. I'm in your debt."

"Name's Jeremiah Branson, and you don't owe me, uh . . . nuthin', Marshal," Jeremiah said, as his eyes suddenly fixed on the badge pinned to Ivory John's vest.

"You live around here, Mr. Branson?"

"Jeremiah. An' I reckon I stay mostly . . . over there," he said, nodding toward a series of low peaks across a wide valley to the west. He turned back to the task of cutting the tawny hide from the cougar.

"Looks to be about a day's ride away."

"Three. Maybe more. Dependin' on whether you gotta wait out a flash flood or renegade Injuns. Where you headed, mister?"

"Lake City. And the name's Morgan. Johnson Morgan."

"Morgan? Where is it you hail from?" Jeremiah said.

"Born and raised in Nebraska, mostly. Why do you ask?"

A sudden scowl came over Jeremiah's face.

"It was in Nebraska that a lawman dropped my baby brother with a bullet from a .44. You're the second lawman I seem to have helped out in the past year or so, but there wasn't no one to step in and save my brother from one of your kind."

"What was the lawman's name?" Ivory John asked.

"Don't really know, only know I got a letter from my ma that Billy had been killed, shot down in the street by a sheriff in some small town west of Lincoln."

"Are you also from Nebraska?"

"Naw. Back east. My brother left home when he was just a kid, and I guess he kinda wandered all over. Somehow he musta wandered into Nebraska. I don't know too much about him, since I was away fightin' the Confederates. I reckon I lost track of him," said Jeremiah, with a regretful slump as he heard himself admit aloud that he'd not been around to help his mother with a younger sibling.

"I take it you didn't go back home after the war."

"I had such a bad feelin' about all the kill-ing and such, I just couldn't face my family and friends with blood on my hands. So, I headed west to take refuge in the moun-tains."

"The war wasn't your fault, Mr. Branson, and you killed because someone was trying to kill you. That's called self-defense, and it's something a man gets used to on the frontier." Ivory John knew something of guilt. He was carrying a lot of it around after letting his father walk into that bank back in North Platte without his tagging along as he'd been asked. He just nodded his head and stared at the ground.

"All I know is that I lost some regard for the law after some damned Nebraska sheriff killed my little brother." Jeremiah groped for words as he struggled to keep control of his emotions. "The letter said he never gave Billy a chance."

"Letter?"

"From one of Billy's . . . friends . . . to Ma."

"When was it your brother got killed?" Ivory John frowned as he searched his memory for the name Billy Branson. Noth-ing. He couldn't recall having heard, or of even reading, the name before. When a law-man kills anyone, other lawmen in the area generally learn of it quickly.

"Four years ago. The letter said the sheriff shot him as he came out of a saloon. Oh, I suppose Ma admitted from time to time that Billy might have beeen a little wild, but he'd never hurt a soul —"

Four years back. Coming out of a Nebraska saloon. And the name Billy. That did ring a bell. Suddenly, he remembered the story and it wasn't going to sit well with a grieving brother. "Fly Speck Billy!" he said.

"What?"

"That's what they called him: Fly Speck Billy. As I hear tell he was bent on gaining a reputation for himself as handy with a gun. He wanted recognition badly. Someone came up with the name Fly Speck Billy because he was small. Billy didn't take to the name at first. But, since it got him the attention he sought, he began to accept it. Your little brother had a fierce temper. That temper was what got him in trouble in the end."

"He *was* small kinda, and sickly. He took after our ma; I remember that much. I suppose we all got a bit of a temper now and again. Ain't seen him nor the family since a year after the war. Been about twelve years. He was just a kid the last time I laid eyes on him. What was he supposed to have done to earn himself a bullet?"

"He'd already been drinking heavily when he went into Parker's Saloon. He'd spent all his money in some other establishment. When he demanded whiskey from the bartender, and wanted it put on account, the bartender refused. Saloon policy. No credit. Billy became furious, drew his gun and shot the bartender squarely between the eyes. Two other patrons tried to disarm the boy, but they too were shot for their efforts. The sheriff was across the street when he heard the shots and came running. Billy burst through the doors and started shooting wildly at anyone he saw. The sheriff shot him. Had no choice." Ivory John hooked his fingers in his gunbelt and leaned back against the boulder. "Four men died that day. Three of them at your brother's hand."

The mountain man saw it in the marshal's eyes. What he'd just been told was the truth. He buried his face in his hands. The crudely written letter his ma had received failed to reveal the whole story. The sensitive giant now understood. Long felt but suppressed doubts surfaced. Somewhere deep in his heart he knew, but couldn't let himself admit, that his little brother might have been something other than the innocent portrayed by his friend. He had taken the boy's side primarily out of a guilt for not being there as the youth was growing up, perhaps to guide him along a straighter path. He sensed the sincerity in Ivory John's voice and felt ashamed he'd let his own assumptions get ahead of the truth.

"I reckon I can only say . . . I'm sorry I jumped to a conclusion without knowin' all the facts."

"No need for any apology, I understand. My father was shot down a few weeks ago by three bank robbers. I've been carryin' a load of hate, myself. If I'm not mistaken, the sheriff's name that gunned down your brother was "Farmer Jim" Douglas, and I doubt he's forgotten the incident, either. Nobody looks kindly on the idea of killing another man, choice or no choice."

"No sir, that I know. Had to kill a man myself a year back. It was that or let him cut down a decent man who'd done him no wrong. That time it was all about gaining a reputation, too, with some fancy gun."

"For a week now, I been chasin' the three men that shot my father. Finally caught up with one of them a few days ago."

"Did you have to kill him?"

"No, but somebody else felt he had to, just to even a score. I understood him too. Some men don't leave you no choice."

Jeremiah nodded but said nothing as he solemnly squatted down beside the carcass once again, wiped the bowie against his deerskin pants, and commenced to finish the task he had started. He had the sad eyes of a man who'd lost something of great value. Something lost forever.

"Tell you what, I'm headed for Lake City," Ivory John said, after several minutes of silence, "what say we ride together? It appears to be near the same direction you came from. That is, if you were fixin' to return home. That be alright with you?"

Jeremiah grunted an affirmative, not stopping to look up. "Reckon that'd be alright."

"Then it's settled. Since you know these mountains better'n I'll ever know 'em, the two of us together'll make better time." It was more than a savings of time that interested the marshal about this solitary man, a man he found intriguing. He hoped that an opportunity to talk between them might answer questions he had concerning this territory he knew little about. Besides, traveling alone through the mountains had already taught him one lesson. Don't.

CHAPTER
TWENTY-FIVE

Gar and Rufe dismounted in front of the Little Nugget Saloon, loosely wrapping their reins around the hitching rail.

"Now listen, Rufe, we're here to find out what we can 'bout the law in this town, not to raise a ruckus. Understand?"

"Sure. Sure, Gar, I'll just watch you and do what you do." Rufe stepped in behind Gar as the two entered the saloon.

"Kin I have a sarsp'rilla, Gar?" Rufe asked like a child begging his father for candy.

"Jus' sit down and shut up. No sarsp'rilla nor nuthin' else. D'you hear?"

"Yeah, Gar, I hear. But I'm thirsty."

"Never mind that for now, you just sit here and keep shut 'til I find what I can about the law hereabouts. We'll eat and drink in a bit."

Rufe pouted but sat at the table where he was told. Gar strolled over to the bar to strike up a conversation with the bartender,

Edgar Fry.

"Beggin' your pardon, bartender, I might be lookin' for a job as deputy. Would you know if the sheriff's hirin'?"

"Don't know, but his office is just across the street on the left. You can ask him yourself," the bartender answered. "Mostly though, Sheriff Tauber seems able to handle the job alone."

"He ain't got no deputies?"

"Nope. Just deputizes some of the townsfolk as the need arises, but that ain't often. Only once last year as I recall."

"This fella Tauber must be some man with a gun to keep a town this size under control," Gar said.

"Good enough, I reckon," Edgar said. "Say, you want a beer or whiskey or —"

Before Edgar could finish his sentence, Gar whisked the Colt from its holster and stuck it inches from the surprised bartender's face, pointed directly at his nose. "He as fast as this?"

"D-don't r-rightly know. I ain't never seen him draw down on nobody as I recall," Edgar stuttered, unnerved by the surprising turn of events.

Gar wore a smirk of superiority on his face as he slowly lowered the Colt and laid it on the bar. The bartender's eyes grew wide as he recognized the rattlesnake inlay. He vividly remembered the days when he'd first seen it just over a year back, along with the painful memories it brought back when it was worn by a man meaner than a snake. He had a feeling Creeg Bedloe and whoever this man was had a lot in common. He shuddered at the thought.

Gar took notice of the bartender's re-action, hastily returned the Colt to its holster, then motioned for Rufe to follow him toward the tall, front doors. He pushed them both open, then looked back over his shoulder at Edgar as they swung closed behind him.

"Sheriff! It's back!" an agitated Edgar Fry blurted out as he burst through the door to the sheriff's office minutes later.

"Calm down, Edgar. What's back?"

"That damnable gun of Bedloe's, that's what. I'd know it anywhere. An' I think its gonna bring more trouble."

"Who has it?"

"Don't know the fella's name. New in town. Slick lookin', with a little mustache and the eyes of a weasel. He came in with a big oaf, kinda simple like. I don't like it. Don't like it one bit," Edgar said as he slid down into a straight-back chair across from the sheriff, wringing his hands.

"Don't sound like the fella I sold it to last year. Did he cause any trouble, threaten anybody?" Tauber asked.

"Welll, not exactly, mostly just asked a lot of questions about you."

Tauber walked to the front window. Directly across the street, Gar and Rufe sat astride their horses. Seeing the sheriff come to the window, Gar touched the brim of his bowler and gave a salute, then gently spurred his horse, and the two of them rode slowly out of town toward the foothills to the north.

"Edgar, it appears you did just what he wanted, for you to come runnin' to me," Tauber said. "I'd say you're right about the trouble too."

"You know them two?"

"No, but they fit the description of the pair I was warned of in a telegraph message I received earlier from a marshal. More'n likely, they're Gar and Rufe Baker."

It was a late afternoon that found Ivory John and Jeremiah topping a rise that formed the easternmost rim of a wide, fertile valley. The hill sloped steeply into an idyllic setting: A green saucer of short grass and jade hued trees with streams that sparkled like silver ribbons through rolling fields where cattle and horses grazed in a vast natural corral, bounded on three sides by granite cliffs, and a deep, rapid stream plying the fourth.

But if this panorama seemed a paradise, the spell was quickly broken by the distant crack of rifles that brought the travelers back to the reality of the quicksilver nature of the frontier. Below, no more than a half mile away, a settler's log cabin was under siege by a small band of Indians.

"Let's get down there. Those settlers look like they could use some help," Ivory John said. He started to spur the black gelding forward in a plan to rush headlong down the hillside, but Jeremiah quickly reached over and grabbed the black's reins.

"Hold up. I know these Utes and we'll need to do some thinkin' before we go ridin' into the thick of that bunch."

"Well, don't take too long thinkin' or there'll be nuthin' left to think about. I see but one rifle returnin' fire from the cabin, and I don't see any dead Indians." The contrasting styles of the two men were becoming apparent, with Ivory John eager to jump into the foray and Jeremiah the one to keep caution company.

Jeremiah stood up in the stirrups, then slowly raised his arm and pointed to a spot below and to their right, by a meandering, shallow creek, the banks of which offered cover from stands of aspen and river birch. "See that shallow ditch snakin' 'round from the creekbed toward the cabin? It goes real close to the back, twixt the log pile and that broke down wagon, yonder. If we keep low along that bank, mebbe we can make it to the back door without bein' spotted by those redskins."

"Lead off, my big friend," Ivory John said, eager to get started.

The two left their horses in a dense stand of cottonwood, at the base of a granite cliff, well out of sight of the marauding Indians. Crouching low, they used all the cover they could find in making their way to the rocky creekbed.

"Keep down and close to the left bank. Those heathens can see a man blink clear across this valley . . . at twilight," Jeremiah whispered.

"I get the idea. Keep movin', I'm right behind you."

Scattered gunfire and savage war whoops kept the usually still air stirred up. The Indians were in no hurry. It was only a matter of time before they finished off whoever was manning the one rifle in the cabin. They would make the defender use valuable ammunition in a futile attempt to halt the inevitable, as they continued to play a cautious game before launching one final onslaught, at which time, they would be victorious. Of that they were obviously confident. The lone defender of that solitary place was no match for fifteen Sharps carbines in the hands of fifteen young bucks, prancing fearlessly about, flaunting their superior numbers.

It was during a pause in the shooting that Ivory John and Jeremiah reached the back of the cabin. It had taken nearly half an hour to cover the few hundred yards, but caution was paramount if they were to succeed in arriving undetected.

The back door to the cabin was sure to be barred or bolted or have furniture stacked in front of it, something to secure that entrance from surprise attack. The very situation that must have brought at least some comfort to the soul inside was now a hindrance to the would-be rescuers. They'd have no choice but to rush the cabin and accept whatever circumstances befell them. The probabilities of their getting shot at by someone, and soon, were increasing rapidly.

"Any suggestions?" Jeremiah whispered back over his shoulder.

"Yes, you go first," Ivory John whispered back.

"I had a hunch you'd say that. Better pray I make it through that door on the first hit or our scalps could be drying on a pole before the night's come on us."

"I'm prayin'. Now let's get goin'."

No more conversation ensued as Jeremiah jumped to his feet and began lumbering toward the door. He hit with such force, the weathered rawhide hinges ripped apart like dry leaves. He and the door both crashed to the floor in an explosion of dust and noise. "Don't shoot! We're here to help!" he yelled. Spitting dirt, he quickly rolled aside in case the person with the rifle hadn't heard his announcement before pulling the trigger.

Ivory John ducked in a split second behind him, gun in hand.

Click, snap, click, snap, click.

The sound came from a corner of the darkened room. There, cocking the hammer on an empty Winchester rifle, then pulling the trigger, over and over, huddled a vacant-eyed young woman. The blank expression on her face was simply a pale mask, a distraction from the numbing fear revealed by her terribly shaking hands. She blinked each time the hammer struck the empty chamber as if her mind had deceived her into thinking the weapon was actually firing. She persisted as a reflex action, the only hope she felt she had left for survival. Death was all around her. She alone had survived the attack. Two dead men lay on the floor, both mortally wounded by Indian bullets that had found their marks during the siege that appeared to have lasted for hours.

Ivory John went to her side and gently took the rifle from her trembling hands. Her arms fell to her sides, though she remained expressionless, saying nothing, resigned to her fate as if she had already suffered more than her mind could comprehend, and, no longer defiant, she seemed ready to die.

Putting an arm around her shoulder, he walked her slowly to the open doorway where she could see him better in the shaft of light that now occupied a bright rectangle on the dirt floor, and thus perhaps comprehend that he was not one of those who had come to kill.

"Ma'am, I'm a US Marshal. My name is Morgan, and my friend and I are here to help you. Don't be afraid." His words came with a calm reassurance, even though his brain wanted to scream out in frustration at the wanton murder that had taken place there that afternoon. He nearly gagged at the smell of death that lay at his feet.

"They're gatherin' for their last hurrah," Jeremiah said, peering through a shuttered window. "We'd best be gittin'. Of course, there's a good chance they'll see us and come followin' after."

"Fortunately, we don't seem to have been detected as yet. It appears they don't know we're here. I may have an idea that will keep it that way," Ivory John answered. He led the woman to an overturned chair near the back door, and turned it upright for her. He squeezed her hand as her eyes found his for the first time. "Just stay right there, everything'll be alright." She nodded slightly that she understood.

"What's your plan? Best it not require too much thinkin' on. We're about out of time," Jeremiah said nervously.

"Get that rifle of yours to the window on the left, I'll set up here in the middle one. When they make their rush, make every shot count. We'll need some dead braves for this to work."

"Okay, but killin' a few Injuns ain't the problem, gettin' away is."

"After they start their assault on the front of the cabin, they'll be damned surprised when two rifles start spittin' death at 'em where only one stood before. I figure they haven't counted any casualties for some time, and that's what I'm depending on — surprise! They'll retreat to the brush to regroup. That's when we get out the same way we came in, takin' the lady with us."

"What's to keep them from followin'?"

"Help me prop these two unfortunate fellas up to the windows. Put their rifles in their hands and stick the muzzles through the opening."

Jeremiah didn't fully grasp the significance of Ivory John's plan, but set immediately to the task, and, presently, two dead sentries once again took their posts in defense of their homestead.

The attack came within minutes, and, as Ivory John predicted, the surprise was immediately evident. Withering gunfire erupted from the previously quiet windows, and in less than two minutes, three confident braves lay mortally wounded from the deadly accurate Henry in the hands of Jeremiah Branson. One more died from Ivory John's Winchester. Two more, badly shot up, crawled back into the brush to die, which wouldn't take long. The great Indian raid lasted less than four minutes and had sent the remaining nine renegades racing for cover, and an opportunity to rethink their strategy.

"Now's our chance, let's move!" Ivory

John said with a lowered voice. "Lead the way. I'll follow with the lady."

Out the back door, out of site of the Ute raiders, sprinted three people in a hurry. The Indians, in complete disarray from their turn of fortune, were too busy regrouping to take notice of the three as they slipped quickly from the back of the cabin.

Reaching the creekbed, the three returned by the same route the two men had come using the natural cover along the bank as they hurried for the horses. Once back at the high point from which Ivory John had first spotted the attack taking place, they stopped long enough to view the action taking place below.

Two Indians had been dispatched to circle the cabin and come in from the rear, an action that was obviously felt unnecessary earlier born of a confidence bolstered by the ineffective resistance they had encountered. Another frontal assault was taking shape as the two rushed the open back door, and just as quickly burst back out, racing around the cabin toward the others, screeching and waving their arms.

The others became very animated as the two continued gesturing wildly. Not one shot was fired as all nine then ran for their mounts, then whipped the ponies to a run in a direction that would take them away from both the homestead and the trail the three happy survivors were to take.

"What happened down there? Why'd they run off like that? I've known these Injuns for years, and I've never known them to run from a fight," Jeremiah confessed.

"Superstition. To our good fortune, we made it out of there without bein' seen by any of the braves. When they rushed the back and found the two men — both obviously dead for some time — manning the rifles at those windows, I hoped they'd figure angry spirits used the bodies of dead white men to do away with six of their brothers and might do the same to the rest of them if they didn't skedaddle. Looks like they took the bait."

"Gotta hand it to you, that was plumb quick thinkin'," Jeremiah said, wiping a sweaty brow with his hand.

"Yes . . . it was. They would have approved," came a soft whisper, the first words either of them had heard from the woman. Her green eyes were now moist, her cheeks streaked with silent tears, tears both of relief and sorrow, the first emotion she'd shown.

"Give me your hand, you can double up with me, ma'am," Ivory John said with a smile. "We'll get you to a safer place."

Slowly reaching for his hand she said nothing as he drew her up behind him on the black gelding. Nearing exhaustion, she slipped her arms around him, rested her head against his back and closed her weary eyes as they rejoined the trail toward Lake City.

CHAPTER
TWENTY-SIX

Eight men gathered around the entrance of the Gold Doubloon mine as Gar and Rufe approached and dismounted. Gar said nothing as he ambled through the bunch of rough, well-armed drifters that Benson had rounded up. None looked much brighter than Rufe, but there'd be no need of any great minds to carry out the plan to extort money from the local miners. He just needed plenty of guns to back him up, and men mean enough to use them. They at least gave the appearance of satisfying that requirement.

"Glad you're back, we're ready to get this plan movin'," Benson called out from the mine entrance, then stepped outside carrying a rifle. "These men can do the job. They're all wanted for somethin' or another, somewhere. They know whats brewin', and they're ready. What happened in town?"

"Nuthin', yet," Gar said, leaning against a

rusting ore wagon to light a cheroot, "but I expect I'll be havin' to git rid of that sheriff, and soon."

"Why's that?" Benson asked.

"The bartender at one of them saloons kept eyein' this Colt, like he'd seen it before."

"Creeg Bedloe!" Benson blurted out, eyes fixed on Gar's sidearm.

"Who?"

"That snake-eyed Colt belonged to Creeg Bedloe. The Lake City sheriff gunned him down right there in the street one mornin' a year back. I never know'd what happened to that gun. How'd you come by it?"

"Never mind. Who was this Bedloe?"

"Just a fella who wanted to be a gunfighter. He was tryin' to build a reputation so's he could get signed up by one of them big outfits down New Mexico way."

"So, that's why that scrawny bartender tore outta there straight for the sheriff soon's we left. Musta recognized the gun and run to tell him. Hmm." Gar brought his left hand to his face and began stroking his thin mustache. His right hand dropped naturally to the Colt as his eyes narrowed in thought.

"What's the problem?" Benson asked.

"That sheriff might just tie me to the stage

where I acquired this gun. If he can, he's got cause to arrest me. Now that the sheriff knows the Baker brothers are here, he may try and put together a posse and come for us. Gotta stop him before he can deputize any of them townsfolk. Let's ride for town," Gar said wasting no time getting to his horse.

The men all scattered to retrieve their own mounts, quickly regathering near the mine entrance. When they were together, Gar led out, Benson just behind him, and Rufe brought up the rear.

"If you kill the sheriff, won't they just git another?" Benson asked.

"It'll take 'em weeks, mebbe months, to convince some fool to pin on that badge, at least as long as we put the devil's fear in 'em."

"Killin' the sheriff ain't gonna be so easy, Gar. Besides, what if he ain't got no stomach for comin' after you?"

"Don't make no difference. Gotta stop him now, before he gets the stomach. What's the matter with you, Benson, afraid of one little ol' sheriff?"

"Mebbe," Benson answered under his breath. "And I don't like the idea of killin' the law."

In a sudden burst of anger, Gar yanked

sharply back on the reins and drew the Colt as he whirled around in his saddle, bringing the gun to within inches of Benson's face. Through clenched teeth, Gar said, "What I say is what gets done! Now, are there any more questions?"

"N-no!" Benson swallowed hard, then broke into a cowardly grin. "Whatever you say, Gar, that's what we do."

Gar holstered the Colt and turned to look for any disagreement from any of the others. No one showed the slightest inclination to argue the point. Satisfied, he spurred his horse to a gallop, and the others followed his lead. By sundown, they would be in Lake City.

Camping by a stream a half-day's ride from Lake City, Ivory John, Jeremiah and the green-eyed girl sat near a fire, built to take the chill off the clear night air, and to cook up the last of Ivory John's coffee.

"We'll be in Lake City tomorrow, ma'am," the marshal said.

"Please call me Amanda, Amanda Pomeroy."

"Amanda. Pretty name," Ivory John said. "Was one of those men back there your husband?"

"No. They were my brothers. My husband,

John Edward, was killed during a stagecoach robbery last year while traveling to Omaha to meet me. He was murdered for his gun collection. They never gave him a chance. I hope I never meet the man face-to-face who did it. I don't believe in killing, but —" She paused, brought a finger to her eye and brushed away the onset of a bitter tear.

"I came out here soon afterward to get away from the memory of his death. Death seems to have followed me." She drew up her legs and wrapped her arms around them, leaning her chin on her knees as she gazed wistfully into the leaping flames. Silky, auburn hair hung in loose curls to her shoulders; high cheekbones, and soft, fair skin revealed a classic beauty that went deep.

"I'm sorry about your brothers. I wish we'd gotten there sooner," Ivory John said. Shyly, he drew circles in the dirt in front of the fire with a brittle, misshapen branch. He hesitated, not quite sure how to approach this woman. She was strong, yet fragile. There was nothing here of the coarse, gaudy saloon women with whom he was so familiar. She had the look of someone born into a world far different from his common beginnings. Uncertain of his own words, he nevertheless knew he must discover what lay beneath that stoic, but beautiful exterior. "Lucky we came when we did, though . . . or I-I'd never gotten to see those pretty, green eyes."

She looked up from the fire. Her eyes sparkled as her sadness became a gentle smile. "Thank you," she said. "You seem to know just what to say to a woman."

"I'm afraid you're about the first one, other than, well, you know . . . ," Ivory John answered shyly, eyes to the ground. "I've never been much with the ladies. Been too busy chasin' outlaws, I s'pose."

"And Indians?"

"Not too many of them, ma'am," Ivory John chuckled.

"Amanda, remember?"

"Yeah, Amanda." He looked up to catch the flame's reflections dancing in her eyes. *Amanda with the green eyes, how could I ever forget?* That look in her eyes brought an unexpected warmth to the chill night air, a warmth he wasn't certain how to address. He decided to take the easy way out. "Better try and get some sleep. We'll be wantin' to get an early start. Here, take this blanket and stay near the fire, you'll be warm enough."

"What will you do if you give me your only blanket?"

"I'll be fine, just fine. I'm used to the night air. Probably spent more nights around a fire under the stars than I have in a bed." He unrolled the blanket and draped it loosely around her shoulders. She took the corners and pulled them tightly around her.

"Thank you," she said, and closed her eyes, still sitting up.

Ivory John added several dead branches to build up the crackling fire before stretching out on the bare ground, legs crossed, head resting against his saddle. Even with his eyes closed, those green eyes wouldn't go away. He thought about how dangerous getting to know her could become, and how being a lawman was hard for some women to understand.

Nearby, Jeremiah snored loudly. He had gulped the hot coffee and without a word, drifted off. The steady whisper of the rushing stream had quickly lulled him to sleep. Looking like a hibernating bear propped against a tree, he was completely oblivious to the others.

Sheriff Tauber watched from his office window as eleven men rode past, stopped in front of the Little Nugget Saloon, dismounted and went inside. At the head of the bunch was the man with Bedloe's gun.

Tauber decided he should find some men to deputize just in case they turned out to be as lawless as they looked. There was a strange odor in the air. It smelled to him like trouble. He drew a rifle from the rack, then closed the door behind him as he headed for the general store one block down, across from the livery.

"Afternoon, Sheriff," a man said from behind the long, merchandise-covered counter. "What can I do for you?" Egan Branfills, a portly Englishman who had come to Lake City only a year and a half before, had been one of the men Tauber had deputized after Simon Stover's death.

"Egan I could use your help, again, as a deputy."

"It's that man with Bedloe's gun, isn't it, Sheriff?"

"Yep. How'd you know?"

"It's all over town. And, I just saw him enter the saloon leading a group of rather unsavory gentlemen." Egan returned to pulling canned goods from a crate and stacking them in neat rows on the shelf behind him. "I'm afraid I'd not be much help against gunmen, Sheriff. I shall have to decline."

"I understand, thanks anyway." Tauber left the store and made his way to the hotel at the end of the street. As he entered, Matt Carver, the desk clerk, came from a back room.

"Howdy, Sheriff," he said. "I hope you're not here for what I think you are."

"That bein'?"

"About them men that rode into town a bit ago."

"You seem to be way ahead of me, Matt. Yeah, I'm needin' deputies. Am I wastin' my time here too?"

"I-I'm sorry, but I got a family, kids, folks countin' on me for support. I would if I could, you understand." Matt hung his head, ashamed of his cowardice, but unable to overcome the fear that had drifted into town with that bunch of gunslingers.

Tauber said nothing as he pushed through the front door, letting it bang against the wall. He did understand, but that didn't make it any easier for him to accept the realization that at some point, he was likely to have to face that bunch alone. The thought was not comforting. He started for the livery and his last chance at finding a willing soul to back him up. Before he reached the front of Johnny Beaver's Livery, Johnny came out and met him in the street.

"Havin' trouble findin' help?" Johnny asked. He knew the answer. He'd seen the dejected look on the sheriff's face as he went from one store to another. Johnny knew, too, what they were all afraid of. He'd seen the men that rode in behind that man in the trailduster. Even to an inexperienced young man in a quiet town in the mountains, a gunslinger is easy to spot.

"Yep." John Tauber sighed and shook his head. "Reckon the idea of runnin' up against that bunch don't appeal to folks."

"I don't know if I can be of any help, but if you got an extra gun, you can count on me."

"Had a feelin' I could. Thanks. Walk down to the jail with me and I'll swear you in and get you armed. Then start prayin' you don't have to use it."

CHAPTER
TWENTY-SEVEN

"Sheriff, they're threatening to beat the tarnation out of one of the girls for refusin' to drink with 'em," the bartender said excitedly as he rushed into the sheriff's office. Sweat poured down his face. He twisted a bar towel in his hands anxiously.

Tauber didn't like what he heard. It sounded like a setup, but he knew he couldn't refuse. What if someone really was in trouble? That was his job. He turned to Johnny, who was sitting on the corner of the desk, eyeing a shiny badge pinned to his wrinkled, gray shirt. "Grab a couple of rifles, Johnny, and make sure they're loaded. Edgar, you git back to the saloon. We'll be there in a spell."

The bartender left without a word, only a quick glance at the floor, an uneasy look on his face — a look that told Tauber to be more cautious than usual.

"Johnny, I want you to go around to the

rear of the Nugget, then, come in the back door and cover me." Tauber stood in the open doorway, pointing to an alley access to the rear entrance to the saloon. "Try to get there without being noticed if possible. I'll give you a couple minutes before I go in the front. And, be careful."

Johnny nodded, then left by the rear of the jail. He ran down the alley behind the livery, crossing the street a block down, then back up the alley behind the meeting hall.

The sheriff snapped open his pocket watch, stared at it for a bit, then replaced it in his vest pocket. It was just before noon. He took his old, sweat-stained hat from a peg near the door, put it on and walked outside, rifle in hand. It was time. Johnny had been gone three minutes. That should be enough time to get in position, he thought. He stepped into the dusty street with a bad feeling in the pit of his stomach.

That very morning, the stage had brought several new dodgers on wanted men. Gar Baker's was among them. One thousand dollars dead or alive it said: Wanted for murder and robbery. He knew he was up against a formidable adversary, a ruthless killer who had chosen this peaceful town upon which to inflict his evil. He just didn't know why?

■ ■ ■ ■

As he reached the back door to the saloon, Johnny twisted the knob slowly, in an attempt to gain entrance quietly and unobserved. Just then, he heard a shuffling sound behind him. He turned and was startled to see a wide-eyed, grinning giant of a man about to encircle his thin body with massive arms. He tried to raise the rifle to a position to fire, but, before he could, he was grabbed in the crushing, bear-like grip of Rufe Baker. In an instant, his breath was forced from his lungs. Before Johnny could make a sound, a huge sweaty forehead came crashing against his face. Johnny's world turned dark as he was released, unconscious, to drop limply to the ground. Blood spread over his face from a broken nose.

Entering the Little Nugget, Tauber found himself face to face with several hard cases, trail dirty and well armed. The usual raucous atmosphere was gone, replaced with a nervous tension among the regulars, all of whom looked like they wished they were somewhere else. One man stepped away from the bar, tossed his empty glass to a man standing nearby, and pulled his trail-duster back to reveal the nickel-plated Colt.

He was a slight man, well dressed in a brown, store-bought suit and bowler hat.

Tauber's eyes went immediately to the ivory inlay on the grips. His thoughts raced back to that same gun, one year earlier, and a similar type wearing it. His stomach tightened as he was brought to the realization that this man was far more dangerous than Bedloe, who, at least, had been predictable. Gar Baker appeared to be anything but. Uneasily, the sheriff stood his ground as Gar took two steps toward him.

"It seems there's some misunderstanding here," Tauber said. He glanced about the room, but saw no woman in trouble as had been reported. He then glanced over at Edgar, nervously wiping and rewiping the same glass over and over, unable to look the sheriff in the eye. Tauber now knew for sure he'd been drawn into a bad situation and his prospects for survival hinged on Johnny Beaver coming through that back door without delay.

"Misunderstanding?" Gar laughed. He threw a sideways glance at Benson who echoed a like response.

"Musta been a mistake, don't seem to be a problem here," the sheriff said, taking a step backward toward the door.

"You know who I am?" Gar yelled at the

sheriff. He couldn't just let the sheriff leave. He aimed to provoke him into making a move. If, when he gunned the sheriff down, he'd done it fair, anyone else in town with an interest in taking Tauber's place would give the idea a hard second thought.

"You seem to fit the description of a wanted criminal and murderer: Gar Baker. Am I correct?"

"You got a sharp eye, Sheriff. I expect you figure on takin' me in for some of my misdeeds. That right?" Gar slid his hand forward then away about two inches from the grips of the Colt, flexing his fingers. He was ready and he wanted Tauber to fully understand that the only way the sheriff was going to leave that saloon was to kill or be killed.

Sheriff Tauber had silently come to the same conclusion that was going through the mind of the gunman he faced. Time was running out. *What the devil had happened to Johnny?* His thoughts were coming too fast. *Should I dive to the floor as I fire? Should I drop the rifle and try to make it to the door while Baker is deciding whether or not to shoot an unarmed man? Should I stall for time? What's happened to Johnny?* Then, all his questions were answered as he saw that telltale twitch in Gar's eye, that half blink

260

that occurs just before a man draws his weapon. Tauber instinctively raised the rifle, pulling the trigger a split second too late. He saw the muzzle flash, heard the roar of that fancy Colt as searing pain tore at his chest. He felt the slug smash into his body. He was thrown backwards by the force of the bullet onto a table near the window, breaking it in half and dumping him, several half-empty whiskey glasses, and a deck of cards to the floor. All sense of what was happening left him as he blacked out, laying motionless in an increasing pool of his own blood.

Gar took several steps toward the seemingly lifeless body, reached down and ripped the badge off the sheriff's shirt, then turned back to the bar. "Drinks on the house, everyone. Any objections, bartender?"

"N-no sir," Edgar knocked over several glasses in the rush to get them lined up in a row, then hurriedly splashed watered-down whiskey into each.

The back door creaked open and a bloody Johnny Beaver stumbled in. He saw the sheriff lying on the floor near the door, crossed the room quickly and knelt down beside the body. His eyes rose slowly to the man who stood not ten feet away, still holding the Colt. Gar confidently holstered the weapon, daring Johnny to make a move to retaliate. There was complete silence as all eyes were on the shaken, half-breed deputy.

"Git him outta here, breed, I don't wanna see him while I drink." Gar snorted, then raised his glass. "To the new law around here," he toasted, pinning the badge on himself. The others followed with a cheer.

Johnny's eyes shot instantly to the gun in the man's holster, a gun he hoped he'd never see again. There was no point in trying to take this madman down against such odds. What chance did he have? Defeated, he took hold of the sheriff's arms and dragged him through the front doors and onto the boardwalk. A crowd quickly gathered around him.

A tall, well-dressed man pushed through the onlookers and leaned over to take the sheriff's wrist. It was the town's new doctor, Benjamin Garfield. He motioned for Johnny to help him lift Tauber's body. "Help me get him over to the jail," the doctor said under his breath.

As they cleared the crowd, Johnny asked, "Why take him to the jail? Shouldn't we just take him to the undertaker?"

"Shhh," the doctor said. "Keep your voice down 'til we get out of earshot of the others." They were near the middle of the street before he finished saying what he'd started. "This man's not dead."

"How'd you know that?"

"I suspected as much when I looked through the window of the saloon and saw the way he was lyin' on the floor. There was blood pumping out of that wound. That meant his heart was still beating. I confirmed that when I took his pulse, weak as it is. Now let's get him inside so I can take a better look at him." The two of them lifted Tauber's limp body onto a bunk in one of the two cells in the back of the jail.

"Get me several clean cloths that I can use to stop this bleeding; then, go over to my office and get my bag. Go by the back way so you aren't seen. When you return, I'll have a look at that nose of yours too."

"Yessir," Johnny said, wiping some of the dried blood from his own face with the kerchief tied around his neck.

"Oh, and Johnny, get back quick, this man's life is depending on it."

"I will, sir." Johnny wasted no time. He left by the back door of the jail, raced through the alley cluttered with discarded trash and crates from the stores along the way, and toward the doctor's office.

CHAPTER
TWENTY-EIGHT

"I'm glad you decided to come on to Lake City with us, Jeremiah," Ivory John said as the three approached the outskirts of the small town.

"Reckon the company didn't hurt me none, either," Jeremiah replied. A mangy, little black and white dog ran along in front of them acting as the town's official greeter and guide. Halfway up the main street, he wearied of his duties and scampered off to bark after a horse and buggy being hastily driven in the opposite direction.

Ivory John, Jeremiah, and Amanda dismounted in front of the livery as they noticed a crowd of people dispersing a block up the street in front of the Little Nugget Saloon. Several people passed by, before one, noticing the marshal's badge, stopped to say something to Ivory John.

"This ain't a healthy town for lawmen today, Marshal," said Matt Carver, the clerk at the hotel. "They just killed Sheriff Tauber, and I don't know what's comin' next."

"Who killed the sheriff?" Ivory John asked.

"Some slick feller named Baker, or somethin' like that. Sheriff never had a chance, what with all them ruffians to backup that stinkin' gunslinger." Matt hung his head as he continued on down the street to the hotel. He kicked at a clump of dirt like a disgruntled kid. He mumbled as he left, "And none but the breed offered help when asked."

"I'd better go to the jail and talk to whoever's in charge now," Ivory John said. "Be obliged for your help, Jeremiah."

"I'll be along," Jeremiah added, "soon's I find that young Beaver fella to bed down our mounts. The jail's nearly across the street from where them folks was gatherin'."

"So, you are familiar with this town?"

"Yep. This is where I gave Sheriff Tauber a hand when he needed it a year ago. I'll do whatever I can to help you get them that shot him, you can count on that."

"Thanks. We may need all the help we can get. Amanda, you go to the hotel and wait 'til we get back," Ivory John said, pulling the Winchester from it's scabbard. "And whatever you do, stay off the streets." He watched after Amanda as she went toward the hotel. Seeing her safely enter the front door, he pulled his Stetson down low in front and began the walk to the jail, a block away. Jeremiah led the two horses inside the livery, calling Johnny Beaver's name.

Finding no one inside, he unsaddled the horses himself, watered and fed each. Then, taking his prized Henry, he retraced Ivory John's footsteps.

Dr. Garfield looked around, startled by Ivory John's unexpected entrance into the sheriff's office. He stepped quickly to the front room. "What do you want here, mister. Th-the sheriff's away."

"I'm US Marshal Johnson Morgan. I hear the sheriff's been murdered, that right?"

"Not exactly," the doctor said, relieved to see a lawman. He turned to reenter the cell where Tauber lay, still unconscious. "I'm Dr. Garfield, and the sheriff's been gravely wounded."

"Will he live?"

"I'm not sure, but I know those men in the saloon wouldn't like it none if they found out he wasn't dead." Dr. Garfield bent over the still figure lying in the bunk. He lifted a blood-soaked cloth from his patient's chest, then replaced it with a clean one. "I've almost got the bleeding stopped, but the bullet's still in there. If he lives, he'll be down for a spell. I do know that."

The back door creaked opened and Johnny Beaver entered, stopping short at the sight of the tall, blond-haired stranger with the bushy mustache.

"It's all right, Johnny. This here's a US Marshal," the doctor said. Johnny took a deep breath.

"What happened, Johnny?" Ivory John asked.

"The sheriff was called to come to the saloon and help git one of the gals outta some trouble. Only when he got there, there weren't no trouble with any of the ladies. It was just them outlaws' way of gettin' him to the saloon where they meant to gun him down. And that's what they did."

"Did you go in with him?"

"No, he sent me 'round back to come in and cover him. Jus' as I was startin' to open the door though, a big, awful lookin' man grabbed me, near choked the life outta me, then he smashed my face with his head. All I remember after that was wakin' up in the dirt with blood all over. Musta been during that time they shot Sheriff Tauber."

"Do either of you have any idea why they wanted the sheriff dead?" He received no answer. Ivory John sat in the swivel chair at the sheriff's desk, shuffled through some of the papers that lay neatly stacked in the center, then pulled one out and read it. He held the poster up for Johnny to see. "Is this the man that shot him?"

"Y-yes! That's him, Gar Baker."

"Baker must have figured the sheriff would try to arrest him if he knew he was in town, and decided to call the sheriff out, to pick his own ground, so to speak." Ivory John leaned on the desk with both elbows, planning just what his response to the day's events was going to be.

"I'm going to need a hand here," the doctor called from the back cell. "Johnny, get some hot water in a pan, and light one of those lanterns. I can use all the light I can get." He placed several of the instruments he took from his bag on the seat of a straight-back chair he'd dragged into the cell. He rolled up his sleeves and began removing Tauber's blood-soaked shirt.

Several minutes later, the glass in the windows across the front of the small building rattled as Jeremiah stepped heavily up on the boardwalk, grasped the knob and pushed the door open wide. It banged against the wall. Johnny was surprised at the sight of the big mountain man, a man he remembered clearly from when Creeg Bedloe tried to gun the sheriff down with the fancy Colt. His friend, Tauber, had survived that face down, but was now on the receiving end of a bullet from the same gun. The sheriff had confided to young Johnny that it had been Jeremiah Branson, the mountain man on the big sorrel mare, who had actually shot Bedloe after the sheriff's rifle jammed. And now that same man stood in the open doorway. How odd that he should have returned to Lake City at such a time as this, Johnny thought.

"The sheriff told me all about what happened, Mr. Branson. That was a great thing you did, saving his life like that."

"Hmm," grunted Jeremiah as he marched across the room, sat down hard on the chair across the desk from Ivory John, then removed his hat and began fanning himself with it.

"If I hadn't given the sheriff that gun of Bedloe's, maybe this wouldn't have happened."

"What are you talking about, Johnny?" Ivory John asked.

Johnny scratched his head, placed his hands in his pockets, and began pacing back and forth across the room. "After Mr. Branson here shot Bedloe, everyone was so excited that such an evil man had been killed, they all went off and forgot about the gun lyin' in the street. I picked it up and kept it. Some time later, a man named Ezra Goode killed Mr. Stover, the owner of the livery stable, and robbed him of all his money. Mr. Stover had took care of me when my ma was killed by Indians. I was obliged to him for everythin', but I was afraid they'd think I done it, so I lit out for the mountains. I didn't know that ol' Ezra had taken the same trail. When I come upon him, about the same time as the sheriff, and I see Ezra's got a clean shot at the sheriff, well, I just pulled the trigger. The ol' man fell over dead. The feelin' you get in the pit of your stomach when they's someone got killed by your own hand ain't somethin' for a body to be proud of, so I give the Colt to Sheriff Tauber to get rid of. He sold it to some fella named Pomeroy."

"Pomeroy?" Ivory John's expression changed from that of mild interest to wide-eyed surprise. "What'd this Colt look like, anyway?"

"It was a beauty. All shiny, nickel-plate, I think, with some white carvin' in the center of the grips that looked like a rattlesnake fixin' to strike," Johnny said.

Ivory John turned to Jeremiah, who had also picked up on the name Pomeroy. "Amanda said her husband collected guns.

That one sounds like somethin' a collector might like to get his hands on. Could be that Gar Baker is the one that killed Amanda's husband. You thinkin' the same?"

"I am. And if she gets wind of it, that spunky little gal's just likely as not to go after him herself," Jeremiah said.

"My thoughts exactly. Until we get the situation under control, we mustn't let her know what we suspect."

"I'm afraid she already knows, *Marshal* Morgan," Amanda said icily, standing in the open doorway, eyes ablaze with an angry intent Ivory John hadn't seen before. "Why would you even think of keeping such a thing from me?" None of them noticed Amanda had silently entered the room.

"I don't want you involved. You could get hurt. These men are killers, desperate killers. They'll let nothing get between them and whatever their reason is for being here. That man lyin' back there on that bunk is hard proof of that," Ivory John said. He hoped his words would convince her of the danger they all faced, but he could tell by her expression that they had fallen on deaf ears. The alluring softness was gone, replaced by the unmistakable presence of the desire for revenge. He knew the feeling well.

"But I *am* involved! I want to help! If that man did kill John Edward, I owe it to his memory to do all I can to help bring that animal to justice." She stood boldly, hands on her hips. The determination in her eyes said much about her character; her words just reinforced it.

She wore the same clothes she was wearing when they found her in that cabin: A much-too-large man's black-and-blue-checkered shirt tucked into a long, gray split-skirt. Long, thin fingers easily managed the curve of her slim waist, around which a rawhide belt reached once, then tucked in under itself to take up the ample excess. A white scarf hung loosely around her neck. Even in the ill-fitting shirt, she was a strikingly beautiful woman, and Ivory John struggled to keep from letting that fact, and his naturally overprotective nature when it came to women, become the basis for his refusal to consider her request to help bring down the Bakers. She was persistent; he, resolute. Oil and water.

"I can't let you get anywhere near that man, Amanda. He'd as soon murder a woman as a man where it serves his purpose. He's done it more than once." Ivory John's disposition revealed that his patience was beginning to wane. Time was not on his side. He saw it as being up to him to put an end to Gar Baker and his gang, and it had to be done soon. Amanda's stubbornness could become an obstacle to achieving that goal.

"I must do something! *You* just don't understand!" she demanded, eyes ablaze and jaw set.

Dr. Garfield broke in. "I could use some of that willingness to help. If I have even a small chance of saving this man's life, it's going to take all the help I can get!" His voice crackled with impatience as he came into the room, and stepped between the two of them. "I'll not be able to get that bullet out with only two hands. Ma'am, would you be willing to put some of that energy into *saving* a man's life?"

The prospect of being needed seemed to ease, if temporarily, the storm that was brewing within her. She nodded her consent and followed the doctor back into the cell. Ivory John silently doubted this would be the last he'd hear of the issue, but eagerly accepted whatever delay the doctor's request might offer.

"Jeremiah, would you consider lettin' me deputize you? I could sure use some help myself."

"Reckon I can't refuse," the mountain

man said with a squint, and a stroke of his beard.

"I let the sheriff down once, I won't let you down if you've a mind for another hand," Johnny Beaver offered.

"Might not be a bad idea at that, Johnny, especially since the sheriff already swore you in. Looks like that makes you acting sheriff." Ivory John motioned for the two to join him around the sheriff's desk. He turned one of the wanted dodgers over to the blank side, pulled a pencil from the desk drawer, and handed it to Johnny. "Johnny, can you draw a map of Lake City? I want to know the most likely route that gang might take if they needed to leave in a hurry. Also, put down where there's good cover, and any large, open areas between the Nugget and the outskirts of town. And, I'll need your help obtaining a few mining supplies, including dynamite. Think you can do all that?"

"Yessir," he said, already setting about the map.

"I smell another of your plans comin' on," Jeremiah observed.

"Hmmm," Ivory John mused as he and Jeremiah hovered over Johnny's quickly progressing map. "Only appears to be two good ways out of town — what with the lake

on one side and mountains on the other —
and only one decent road. If they was to
run, the most likely way'd be up here,
toward Cannibal Plateau. We need to guarantee they'll be thinkin' the same."

CHAPTER
TWENTY-NINE

Gar cleared the saloon of all but his own men. He called them all together around a table near the back, and began to lay out his plan for their eventual control of the entire valley and all the mining operations nearby. "With that sheriff out of the way, the smaller mines will have no one to look to for protection. They'll have to pay or fight. They'll pay. They'll not have the stomach for a gunfight after they hear I gunned down their sheriff. And that's something we got to let 'em know. Benson, that'll be your job, since they all know you." Gar stood at the center of the group as they silently listened to him give his instructions. Not one had a question when asked. They all smiled and nodded to each other. This kind of treachery appealed to them. Benson had picked his crew well.

"Benson, take two men, ride out and spread the news. The rest of us'll stay here and make sure this one-horse town don't get no ideas about gettin' some backbone," Gar ordered.

Benson pointed to two men and left immediately. "Simms, you ride north. Dover, you take the east and I'll go south. Don't have to hit but the first few mines you come to, they'll tell each other for sure. Be back here by midnight," he said, mounting his horse.

"Marshal, I just saw three of 'em leavin' the saloon, each ridin' out in a different direction," Jeremiah said, standing at the window. "I think it might be a good idea to follow one of 'em, find out what they're up to?"

"Go to it. But, be careful. Can't afford to lose you."

"You just don't want to lose this Henry," Jeremiah snorted as he slipped out the door and headed for the livery and his horse. He'd decided to follow the man riding south.

Johnny had not yet returned with the supplies he'd been sent for; so, Ivory John went back to the cell to see what he could do to help the doctor and Amanda. "Any way of knowin' yet if he'll make it, Doc?"

"Well, the bullet's out, and the bleeding's stopped. From here on out, it's going to be wait and see. He lost a lot of blood. I don't give him a very good chance, but, he's strong." He stood up, stretched his back, then pulled a towel from the back of the chair and wiped his hands. "This young lady was a great help. Couldn't have got him this far without her."

Amanda brushed a strand of wandering hair out of her eyes with the back of her hand, then, without a word, walked straight to the window, and stared gloomily at the saloon. "Are they still in there?" she asked.

"Most of 'em," Ivory John answered.

"What do you plan to do?" she asked.

Ivory John knew he had to be careful not to give her too much information for fear she'd find a way to get in the middle of the action. "I'm workin' on a little surprise."

"Meaning —"

"Meanin' I'll let you know when it's set."

"Well, you'll find me at the hotel when that time comes," she said abruptly.

"Amanda, I only want to keep you safe."

She didn't acknowledge his last comment as she brushed by him, through the door into the warm afternoon sun. On the way to the hotel, she stopped at the general store to purchase something she'd noticed displayed in a wood-framed case in the window: A .41 caliber Remington double derringer.

■ ■ ■ ■

Long, fingery shadows followed the contours of the rugged terrain, signaling the waning afternoon hour. Even in the dimming light, Jeremiah had no trouble tracking Benson without being seen. The old man hadn't the least suspicion he was being followed.

After Gar's lieutenant left the first mine he came to, Jeremiah rode out from behind a rocky rise where he'd reined-in to keep from being spotted. Seeking the reason for Benson's visit, Jeremiah rode up on three miners who stood staring after the departed rider. One of the men wheeled about, awkwardly attempting to arm himself with his handgun as Jeremiah rode up.

"We already got the message from your friend there, so you can just keep on ridin'," one said.

"I ain't with him. I just want to know what he come for." Jeremiah sat his saddle, hands stacked on the pommel. He made no move toward the Henry tucked in the scabbard. "I mean you no harm," he assured them.

The man released his grip on the revolver he carried high on his side, and stepped closer to Jeremiah's big sorrel. "He brought some unsettlin' news. Said a top gunslinger killed the sheriff, and his bunch'd be protectin' our interests from now on. Called it a safety committee," the man said angrily. "They'll be takin' a fee for —"

"Never mind, I get the idea. Don't worry none, a US Marshal's come to town, and he'll not let this pack of wolves feed on you miners. Besides, the sheriff ain't dead. Least ways, he wa'nt when I left town." Jeremiah pulled the reins hard to the right and spun the sorrel around to return to Lake City. He knew all he needed to know. He urged the big horse to a run.

As the day waned cloudy and cool, the town was full of miners from the surrounds, in town to purchase supplies, and then settle in for a few rounds at a saloon before returning to their diggings. Ivory John was busy setting his plan into motion. Johnny had returned with the items the marshal had requested: A case of dynamite, a miner's pick, shovel, hammer and nails, a roll of barbed wire and a bolt of red flannel.

"What're you gonna do with all this stuff, Marshal?" Johnny asked.

"We're settin' out to make a box canyon out of this open area here, where the main street joins this wagon trail up to Cannibal Plateau," the marshal said, pointing to a spot on the map Johnny had drawn. "Soon as its dark, we'll set to doin' it."

Just then, Jeremiah burst through the door at the rear of the jail, half out of breath. "Well, them hombres is fixin' to charge a big fee to all the miners in the area. They're calling it protection. I call it a holdup. That's why they had to shoot Sheriff Tauber, so's he couldn't get in their way."

"Extortion."

"What?" asked Jeremiah.

"What they're doin' is called extortion. And we've got to stop them before they can get started."

"Whatta you got in mind?"

"Gather around and I'll show you. First, Johnny, you've got to get someone you can trust into the saloon to give that bartender this message," Ivory John said, handing Johnny a folded piece of paper. "Do you think we can trust him?"

"If he ain't too scared, we can."

"That note ought to bring him a little courage. Now, very late tonight, the three of us are going to dig a few holes and bury some dynamite," — he pointed to the map — "here, here and here. We'll tear this flannel into strips, wrap the strips around bundles of three sticks of dynamite each. Leave about six inches loose so it'll stick up above the ground. Jeremiah's gonna have to see the red clearly so he can hit it with the Henry from his position on the balcony of this buildin', here."

"Why's he gonna do that?" Johnny said, scratching his head.

"The three of us can't take on that whole bunch by ourselves, we're gonna need some help. The confusion that'll come when those sticks of dynamite go off all around Gar's riders will be our ace in the hole."

"It's a good plan, Ivory John. But, what happens when they just cut through to the alley by goin' between the buildings?" Jeremiah asked.

"That's where the barbed wire comes in. We're gonna build some fences between these six buildings, here, here and here. We'll just nail up a few strands and any horse and rider that tries to cut through will be trapped. I'll be positioned here, at the head of the street. Johnny, you'll set up here, behind them, with a shotgun. That suit you?"

"Yessir. An' thanks for the chance to square things for the sheriff."

"What makes you think they'll ride out that way?" Jeremiah asked.

"If all the players do their part, it's logical that the Baker boys will take their men out of town first thing in the morning, and this route is the quickest way out."

"I sure hope you're right," Jeremiah nodded. "But, what's to keep them from headin' south?"

"Is that where this note comes in, Marshal?" Johnny asked.

"That's right, Johnny. Now, do you think you can get that note to the bartender?"

"You can count on me, Marshal. I got a friend that I think can get it to him," he said. Eagerly, he took the folded paper and slipped out by the rear door, disappearing quickly.

Coming from the cell where Tauber lay, the doctor walked to the desk, and opened several drawers until he found a half-empty bottle of whiskey. "Join me, gentlemen?" he asked.

"No, thanks," they both said together.

"It's early to be speculating on such a thing, but I'm beginning to think he might just make it. We'll know better in the morning. He seems to be getting stronger, though."

"That's good news, Doc. We hope to give him a welcome-back party about that time," Ivory John said, smiling as he pried open the lid to the box of dynamite. "Let's get the candles ready, Deputy Branson."

CHAPTER
THIRTY

Dark had overtaken the little mining town as a young woman with heavy mascara and wearing a low-cut, glistening satin dress made her way through the smoke-filled saloon to the bar. She went directly to the end where the bartender, Edgar, was pulling bottles of whiskey from a wooden crate, stacking them neatly on a shelf behind the bar. A tightly folded piece of paper resided in a small, beaded purse carried in her right hand. As she pried open the purse with long, painted fingernails, to pull out the note with which she'd been entrusted to give to the bartender, a drunken miner grabbed her about the waist, swinging her around. Torn unexpectedly from her grip by the force of his move, the purse and its contents went sailing across the floor, sliding under a table of men playing cards. She struggled to loose herself from the foul-smelling man's grip to regain possession of her property, but, against all attempts at freedom, was danced across the floor to the tinny rhythm being pounded out by a lively piano player.

One of the men at the table kicked the purse with his boot, dislodging the note which now lay in plain view of several miners raising their glasses to a better day tomorrow. The piece of paper caught the eye of Matt Carver, who, trying to drown his guilt at having let the sheriff face Gar Baker alone, found himself uncharacteristically drawn to the town's seamier side. Curious, he bent down, picked it up, and unfolded it under a lamp on the wall next to the bar. He was sober enough to understand the significance of the words written on that innocent-looking piece of paper. Quickly refolding it, he looked around to see if anyone was watching. No one was. He stepped up to the bar and handed the note to Edgar Fry, to whom it was addressed. The two of them went to the far end of the bar to confer quietly.

"What do you make of this, Edgar?" Matt asked. "I found it on the floor. Looks as though whoever meant to give it to you got a little careless."

"Hmm," Edgar said as he read, "I wonder if this is a trap?"

Looking about the room, Matt could see all of the Baker gang. None seemed to be paying any attention to his conversation. "If that bunch of cutthroats had anything to do with it, they'd be eyein' us like an eagle."

Just then, the fancy lady came up to the two of them. "Edgar, I was supposed to give you a note from that young deputy. I lost it. What'll I do?"

"Matt here stumbled upon it by sheer luck. You say you got this note from Johnny Beaver?"

"That's right. He give it to me himself."

"Then it must be on the up and up," Matt said.

"That bein' the case, it looks like a way to rid ourselves of that buzzard with the fancy gun. I'm going to do as the writin' says. Will you back me, Matt?" Edgar asked.

Matt stared at the floor, shaking his head. "I can't let another friend down. I'll do whatever you say."

"Okay, then, when I tell Baker what I'm supposed to, you act like you know what I say is the truth." The two eased back toward the other end where Gar Baker and his brother talked loudly with two of their kind. Edgar placed a newly opened bottle of whiskey on the bar, leaned over and said, "Mr. Baker, there's somethin' I think you should know."

"What's that?" Gar said, turning away from Rufe and the others.

"The sheriff figured you'd be back after you rode outta here the first time, that's when he done it. I'm just tellin' you because you and your boys have been good payin' customers."

"When he done what?" Gar frowned at the intrusion.

"That's when he telegraphed for a posse of lawmen from Durango. They're supposed to be ridin' in from the south come daybreak."

Gar's hand shot across the bar and brusquely grasped Edgar by the shirt front, yanking him forward — hard. "You're lyin', and for less, men have got killed."

"Uh, h-he ain't lyin', uh, sir," Matt broke in. "I was at the telegraph office when the sheriff done it."

Gar released his grip on the hapless Edgar Fry, and drew the shiny Colt. Without hesitation, he fired it twice into the ceiling. The saloon fell dead silent. "Ever'body out. The saloon's closed." Amid the grumbling and griping of the regulars, Gar pointed the gun into the crowd to enforce his edict should any doubt his sincerity. None did, and the place cleared of all but his gang within seconds.

"What's up?" asked Rufe.

"Never mind, just all of you be ready to ride at first light," Gar answered for all to hear. "We'll be leavin' town for a few days."

He picked up the full whiskey bottle from the bar, strode toward a table in the back, leaned back in a creaky captain's chair and commenced to drink down one shot after another. When Rufe tried to join him, the big man was gruffly told to go sit by the front door to keep an eye out for unwanted visitors. Gar didn't really expect anyone to have the nerve to enter after he had chased them out with the promise of eleven guns to greet them if they came back. In fact, he was quite surprised when the doors swung open, and there in the dim light stood a beautiful auburn-haired woman.

"I'm looking for Mr. Baker. Does anyone know where I can find him?" Amanda asked.

"What do you want him for?" a raspy voice answered from a table at the far back.

"I just want to ask him a question, that's all," she said. Her voice was calm, deceptively inviting.

"C'mon back, we'll talk," Gar said. He kicked a chair away from the table as an invitation to sit. She obliged him, laying her ruffled, cloth purse in front of her. She was no longer dressed in the frontier clothes in which she had arrived. Instead, she wore a blue gingham dress, tight at the waist, with ruffled sleeves. Just a hint of red rouge glistened on her full lips. A silver comb held her pulled-back hair. Gar's curiosity was piqued as he asked, "And, just what is it you want with me?"

"I hear you carry a very fancy gun. If that's true, I'd like to see it."

"Now, why would a pretty lady want to look at some ol' gun?" His eyes narrowed with mistrust. Even so, this beauty that sat across from him had his interest aroused, and he eased the Colt from its holster, placing it on the table. "This what you want to see?"

"Oh, yes. It's just like the one my husband wrote me about. It even has the ivory inlay of a snake with ruby eyes." She moved her hand slowly to the open purse.

"Your husband? Was he —"

"— brutally murdered trying to protect his gun collection? Yes! But you already knew that!" Amanda drew the derringer from her purse and aimed it at Gar's head. "*You're* the animal that killed him, aren't you? That's the question I wished to ask. But, you don't seem to have an answer. No matter, you're going to die for it, anyway."

Shakily, she pulled the hammer back to fire.

She jerked the trigger just as a giant hand emerged from behind, savagely grabbing her wrist. As the gun discharged, the bullet missed Gar's head by inches, so close he was temporarily blinded by the flash. Rufe stood holding her wrist in a vice grip, and she winced as his grasp brought tears to her eyes. A terrible realization came over her — her arm had been broken by Rufe's sudden, powerful grasp. The derringer fell harmlessly to the floor as she lost all feeling in her fingers.

"What you want I should do with this here little filly, Gar?"

"Filly? Hell, little brother, that's a full-growed, wild mustang. And I think I know just what to do with her," he laughed. "We'll just take her with us when we ride out in the mornin'. She'll make a good hostage, and more'n fair passage outta here."

Grinning with a depraved respect for his brother, Rufe released his hold on her arm. Amanda nearly fainted from the rush of pain as blood began to circulate again. She cradled the broken arm in the other, drawing it close to her body in hope of relieving the intense throbbing. To no avail. A tear crawled down her powdered cheek.

The seriousness of her situation now

became evident. Her head was swimming with pain, fear and self-recrimination. Why hadn't she stayed out of it like she'd been told and let the marshal handle things? On more than one occasion her husband had scolded her for her bull-headedness, as he called it. Her mother dismissed her obstinate nature as a child as just being a little tomboyish, nothing more. Well, this time, it looked like "nothing more" might get her killed.

CHAPTER
THIRTY-ONE

Ivory John stayed well back in the dark shadows of Mrs. Granville's boarding house at the top of Main Street, where the road made a Y — the open area marked by small telltale patches of red flannel growing out of several small, freshly covered mounds in the rutted dirt. Dawn was just about to break.

Jeremiah yawned and stretched, then waved the Henry in the air as a signal to the marshal that he was in place on the narrow second-floor balcony of the building across the street. A half-block down, hidden behind several barrels of nails on the porch of the hardware store, crouched Johnny Beaver, a loaded shotgun clutched tightly in his hand. By his feet lay a leather bag with two dozen more shells. Nervously, he anticipated the coming action.

They all awaited some sign that Gar and his gang had taken the bait, *if,* indeed, the bait had been delivered, and *if* the bartender had mustered the courage to go through with what he'd found written in the note. *If.* Too many ifs. But then, they shouldn't have to wait long to know for certain.

Ivory John pondered all the possibilities, including why Amanda had given up her quest so easily. He hadn't seen her since the previous day. Having not told her of his plan, he felt confident of her safety. He would certainly know if the circumstances were otherwise, wouldn't he?

The sound of horses slowly approaching from the direction of the saloon echoed off the wooden buildings in the still morning air. That could be them, he thought, but they were not yet in sight. He made a last check of his rifle, then glanced up at the balcony to assure himself that Jeremiah also heard the advancing horses. A slight dogleg in the street would keep the advancing horsemen from view until the very last moment, then, there would be only seconds before they would be in a perfect position for the ambush. The three lawmen must be careful not to strike too early, or the gang could easily escape back in the direction from which they had come; too late, and the Bakers would find nothing to impede their race for open country.

The night had been a busy one, digging holes for the bundles of dynamite, each placed to explode with maximum effect. All side escape routes were blocked, secured with barbed wire nailed across the backs of several buildings. Two experienced riflemen stationed strategically to cut down those with any fight left in them after the smoke cleared. It was a good plan. Nothing should go wrong. The first rays of daylight broke across the false-fronted buildings on the west side of the street.

The lead horse came into view. Gar Baker. It had worked. Ivory John lifted his rifle, preparing to squeeze off the first shot, the signal to Jeremiah to blow the first mound of dynamite. He had drawn a precise bead on Gar himself when a sick feeling in the pit of his stomach overcame him. He broke out in a cold sweat for there, on a second horse, being led by Gar, was Amanda. *Amanda? What the heck? How did she fall into Gar's hands? Now what do I do? If I wait, I'll lose him; if I shoot, she could be hurt, or —* . But, he couldn't think of that. He had only seconds to make a decision, they were just about to the point where the plan called for the first detonation. His killing Gar was now imperative. His aim would have to be perfect, he knew that. He would then have to make a dash into the midst of the melee that was to come, find Amanda and lead her to safety without being shot or blown to kingdom come.

He squeezed the trigger, the hammer fell, but Gar's sorrel became the spoiler. The horse, frightened when a strip of the red flannel directly in front of him began to blow about in a sudden breeze, shied to the left just as Ivory John's rifle echoed down the quiet street with a fiery crack. The unfortunate animal took the bullet intended for Gar and dropped head-first, throwing the surprised gunman into the street just as a mound fifteen feet away exploded with a deafening roar. The marshal's shot — the signal Jeremiah awaited before exploding the first mound with his deadly aim — set off the chain of events that, for the next four minutes, would make Lake City a reasonable recreation of the battle at Shiloh.

The ear-shattering explosion, like a cannon on the line, brought rifles and six-guns blazing away at anything that moved through the smoke, dust, and uproar. Horses went crazy in terror, bucking their riders off, racing about in confused circles as the second blast erupted, spewing dirt, stones and dust thirty feet in the air.

Bringing up the rear of the column,

several lengths behind the rest, Benson avoided the effects of the initial blast. Instinctively, he wheeled his horse around to escape the trap. As he did, he caught sight of the big mountain man on the balcony. Dismounting as he reined-in, he slapped his old bay mare on the rump, sending him back in the direction he'd come from, then made a dash for the shadowed side of the feed store. He took up a position that gave him a clear shot at Jeremiah. Excitedly, he raised his rifle, and centered his sights.

BLAAMM!

A look of shock overcame his face as he was slammed against the building. His short, bowed legs buckled under him as he slid down the clapboard siding, the life oozing from his body, dying eyes wide open in disbelief.

Shaking, Johnny Beaver stood over the still, old man, both shells expended in his still-smoking shotgun. It had been the second time in Johnny's young life he'd had to kill one man to save another. It didn't feel any better than it had the first time, but somehow the badge seemed to make the circumstances more tolerable.

Gunfire spewed out in all directions, as the gang was unable to see or fix on any target. Jeremiah picked off two as they struggled to get to their feet. One was killed when his horse, felled by a stray, rolled over on its ill-fated rider.

Cutting one man down who came at him through the dust blazing away with a six-gun, Ivory John ducked and dodged through the shootout making his way to where he'd last seen Amanda. She was nowhere to be found.

Four of the bunch ran blindly into the barbed-wire traps and were quickly captured by Johnny and Jeremiah. None felt lucky enough to go against a shotgun and that deadly Henry. After the dust settled, the three lawmen could account for all but two outlaws. And one woman.

Ivory John frantically called out to her. After the first explosion, he temporarily lost his bearings. He was knocked off his feet by the second eruption as he made his way to the spot she was last seen, finding to his dismay that not only was she not there, neither were Gar and Rufe. The two he most wanted had somehow managed to slip through the trap, apparently taking Amanda with them.

"Johnny, take these four to the jail and lock them up. Jeremiah, I've a hunch Gar and Rufe might have headed for the livery, since Gar is without a horse, and it's too early for there to be any tied in the street for him to steal," the marshal said. He was already making hurried tracks toward the stables. "I'll go in the front, you come in the back. Remember, they've probably got Amanda, and neither of them seem to have any qualms about killing women."

Jeremiah nodded and lumbered off.

As Ivory John reached the front of the livery, he found one of the doors standing half open, and thinking more with his heart than with his head, he rushed inside, rifle at the ready. The contrast between the bright daylight outside and the near-dark inside temporarily left him blinded. His eyes never got a chance to adjust before his head exploded with a sudden, sharp pain, then total blackness. Rufe had hit him from behind with one mighty swing of a single-tree.

"D-did I do the right thing, Gar?"

"You sure enough did, little brother," Gar grinned evilly. "Now that our plans seem to be changed, thanks to this meddlesome feller."

"What do we do now, Gar? What? What?" Rufe's eyes were wide in anticipation of whatever Gar had in mind, though he had no idea of what that was.

"We'll be usin' the little lady here as a

hostage, to get us clear of this damned town," Gar said through gritted teeth.

Gar leaned over Amanda as she huddled against a pile of straw in the back of a stall, almost in shock. He reached down, took hold of her arm and started to yank her to her feet. She cried out in pain from her broken arm. She kicked at him in vain. He laughed loudly as he squatted on her legs and began to slap her across the face. Awkwardly, he put his hands on her shoulders to shake her so she wouldn't fall into unconsciousness from the pain of her broken arm.

Weak and vulnerable, she had only her left arm free to attempt any sort of defense. Then, as she weakly flailed about, seeking anything to use in warding off her attacker, her hand fell to the grip of the Colt he wore tied down. She tugged at it unsuccessfully, the leather thong that secured it was taught. She dug at the strap with her fingernails until they bled, then, unexpectedly, it gave way as she pushed against the grip, itself, releasing the tension it held against the hammer. The gun slid free of the holster and onto the ground, unnoticed by the man on top of her with nothing more on his mind at that moment than to beat her senseless, probably to keep her from being troublesome as he used her as a shield to make his escape. The pleasure he took in seeing her fear revealed the total depravity in this murderous outlaw.

Frantically, blindly, with her one free hand, she scratched at the dirt and straw on the floor to find that weapon, her last chance, the only thing that lay between her and the pain.

Amanda's muffled screams were the first sounds Ivory John heard as he came to. Dazed and groggy, he fought to ward off the confusion that gripped his aching head. *Amanda is in trouble, but, where? Who?* The fog in his brain seemed too thick to penetrate. He rolled over on his back, staring at the ceiling, and then at the monster that stood nearby looking off into the dim light, rocking back and forth. *Rufe! This beast is Rufe Baker! But, why is he standing there and why am I on this dirt floor?* Slowly, it was all coming back. Along with the ache in his head, his predicament was becoming clearer. He rolled painfully onto his side, in search of Amanda. His hand fell to his holster. Empty. His rifle was nowhere to be seen, either.

Then, when his eyes found her, rage boiled up inside him like the birth of a volcano. He knew he would have to get by

Rufe to have a chance at Gar. He eased up on his hands to make his move on the big man, when —

Gar's mouth turned up in a lusting, expectant grin as he fed off the stark terror in Amanda's eyes.

CRAACK!

The blast of the Colt filled his ears. His body jerked with searing pain as the bullet ripped through his side, flattening as it smashed ribs and severed arteries, filling his lungs with gushing blood. With a howl, he rolled away from her. Making a wide swing of his arm, he knocked the gun from her hand, then made a desperate lunge for it.

Rufe, stupefied by the turn of events, took a giant step toward Gar. "Gar, what should I do? Sh-should I kill her? Gar? Tell me what to do, Gar!"

With his lungs filling with blood, Gar gasped for air, unable to speak. Rufe, near panic, grabbed for the shotgun that leaned against the outer support of the stall, and, shaking, thumbed the hammers back.

Seeing this, Ivory John mustered all the strength he could as he made a dive for Rufe, who went down with a thud and a groan as Ivory John threw his full weight against the back of the big man's massive legs. Then, looking quickly around for any kind of weapon he could use on this beast who was about to rise up and take his retribution with that shotgun, Ivory John spotted the answer. There, on the floor where Rufe had fallen, lay the big man's bowie knife. It had slipped from its sheath as he went down.

The marshal dove for the huge knife, and, grabbing it, jumped to a half crouch as Rufe arose with an angry growl, turning toward him with the shotgun. Realizing he would only get one chance at his defense, Ivory John brought his arm around in a wide, circular motion to gain momentum, and, with one powerful thrust, sank the bowie deep into Rufe's soft upper belly. The giant staggered back, eyes bulging at the sight of the deer-horn handle protruding from him, squealing in anguish as blood gushed from the wound. He dropped the shotgun as he floundered and fell forward, crashing to the floor dead.

Gar reached the Colt just as Jeremiah came bursting through the rear of the building. The mountain man saw Gar raise the shiny revolver in Ivory John's direction and jerk the hammer back. Jeremiah fired from the hip. Gar Baker made no sound as he was spun to the floor, dead from a rifle bullet to the head.

Ivory John stumbled to Amanda's side. He quickly grabbed her limp body in his arms and lifted her off the cold, dirty floor. "Jeremiah, go get the doc, quick!"

Jeremiah was already on a dead run out of the livery stable.

CHAPTER
THIRTY-TWO

Two days later, Ivory John and Jeremiah entered the sheriff's office to find Johnny sitting at the desk, feet propped up, looking very much the deputy.

"Understand the sheriff will survive his wound; that's good news," the marshal said.

"Sure is. He's asked me to stay on as deputy 'til he gets back on his feet. That shouldn't be too hard after you fellas cleaned up most of the troublemakers all at once," Johnny said. "Will you be stayin' for a spell?"

"Mr. Branson and I will be ridin' on to Arizona as soon as we're sure Mrs. Pomeroy will be okay," Ivory John answered.

"Well, if you change your mind and decide to stay longer, I'd sure be obliged for the help."

"You drew your share of the gunfire, Johnny. You'll do fine without any help."

"Thanks, Marshal."

"Just don't pick up any more guns out of the street," Jeremiah chuckled as they left.

Within a week, Amanda was feeling well enough to leave her room. Doc Garfield had set her broken arm with an assurance that within six weeks she'd be good as new. Ivory John had bought her new clothes: A dark green gingham would match her eyes perfectly, he'd decided. She was charmed with his choice.

He was, however, somewhat uneasy as they sat by the edge of the lake in a buckboard from Johnny's livery. She had asked him to take her to the lake's edge the very day the doctor said she could get out of bed. So, Ivory John picked her up at the hotel, and, as Jeremiah followed on horseback, rode the bumpy trail to the lakeshore.

"I-I'm very grateful the two of you came along when you did. I owe you my life for the second time," she shyly broke the silence, "Though, I guess I got myself . . . into the situation in the first place?"

Ivory John raised his eyebrows in a knowing way.

"You needn't say anything, I know I did. But, it has —"

"— seemed to work out all right," he finished, with a smile.

"Well, almost."

"Almost?"

"There is one more thing I'd like you to do before I can put this all to rest."

"What would that be?" he asked.

"Take this and throw it as far out in the lake as you possibly can." She pulled the Colt Peacemaker from beneath a blanket on the seat, and handed it to him. Something in her voice told him he had no choice.

He held the gun in his hand, feeling the perfect balance. He ran his fingers over the fine ivory inlay, momentarily considering the beautiful craftsmanship that had gone into the creation of such a fine instrument — albeit, an instrument that was now being blamed for several deaths. It was condemned to the bottom of the lake forever just for just having been created. A fine instrument, he thought, what a shame.

"Seems a great waste to just throw away a fine piece of workmanship like this," he said.

"Perhaps, but think of all the people who died from having come in contact with it, beautiful or not," she said sadly. "That was a waste too."

He knew destroying the Colt was the only thing she'd accept, the only way she had of letting go of her sorrow over the loss of her husband, and the pain she'd endured at the hands of a depraved outlaw. He had no choice but to accommodate her wishes. He stood up in the buckboard and heaved the revolver well out into the lake. Over and over it tumbled, flickering from the sunlight reflecting off the shiny nickel plating with each turn, until it slashed into the rippling waters to disappear forever into the lake's muddy bottom.

"Thank you," she said, "at least I'll know that no one else will ever again fall victim to *that* gun." She turned to him with a look of renewed strength. "What will you do now? Will you be leaving?"

"I-I reckon."

"I'll, I mean, we'll all miss you. Where will you go?"

"Arizona territory. There's been a minin' boom down there and all that money makes for sizable disagreements between them that has it and them that don't." He ran his fingers through his long, blond hair. He frowned at the thoughts that were going through his head. He really didn't want to leave her, stubbornness and all. Those green eyes had taken a mighty toll against his intention to stay single. Marriage was an attachment that could only bring problems to a career lawman, problems that more than once had come between a man intent on upholding the law at any cost, and a wife that also needed attending to.

With giant hands stacked on the pommel, wondering whose resolve would win out, Jeremiah sat silently in the saddle carefully taking stock of them both. He sensed her interest in the rangy marshal, and that she might welcome a chance to settle down with him. Ivory John's expression showed confusion, some inner struggle, and a waning determination to remain free. A subtle smile crept across Jeremiah's bushy face as he realized Arizona may have to wait just a bit.

The employees of Thorndike Press hope you have enjoyed this Large Print book. All our Thorndike and Wheeler Large Print titles are designed for easy reading, and all our books are made to last. Other Thorndike Press Large Print books are available at your library, through selected bookstores, or directly from us.

For information about titles, please call:
    (800) 223-1244

or visit our Web site at:
    http://gale.cengage.com/thorndike

To share your comments, please write:
    Publisher
    Thorndike Press
    295 Kennedy Memorial Drive
    Waterville, ME 04901